I0831585

The Ridge

A Land Grant Protest Turns Deadly

A Luke Jackson Thriller

The Ridge

A Land Grant Protest Turns Deadly

A Luke Jackson Thriller

PETER EICHSTAEDT

Santa Fe

© 2023 by Peter Eichstaedt
All Rights Reserved
No part of this book may be reproduced in any form or by any electronic or mechanical means including information storage and retrieval systems without permission in writing from the publisher, except by a reviewer who may quote brief passages in a review.

Sunstone books may be purchased for educational, business, or sales promotional use.
For information please write: Special Markets Department, Sunstone Press,
P.O. Box 2321, Santa Fe, New Mexico 87504-2321.

Library of Congress Cataloging-in-Publication Data

Names: Eichstaedt, Peter H., 1947- author.
Title: The ridge : a land grant protest turns deadly : a Luke Jackson thriller / Peter Eichstaedt.
Description: Santa Fe : Sunstone Press, [2023] | Summary: "Convinced he has the story of a lifetime to boost his sagging career, journalist Luke Jackson is caught in an historic land dispute in northern New Mexico that could cost him his life"-- Provided by publisher.
Identifiers: LCCN 2023034046 | ISBN 9781632935342 (paperback) | ISBN 9781611397185 (epub) | **ISBN 9781632936370 (hardcover)**
Subjects: LCSH: Journalists--New Mexico--Fiction. | Protest movements--New Mexico--Fiction. | Land grants--New Mexico--Fiction. | New Mexico--Fiction. | LCGFT: Thrillers (Fiction)
Classification: LCC PS3605.I35 R53 2023 | DDC 813.6--dc23/eng/20230802

LC record available at https://lccn.loc.gov/2023034046

WWW.SUNSTONEPRESS.COM
SUNSTONE PRESS / POST OFFICE BOX 2321 / SANTA FE, NM 87504-2321 /USA
(505) 988-4418

※PREFACE※

Treaty of Guadalupe Hidalgo, 1848, between the United States and Mexico

ARTICLE VIII

Mexicans now established in territories previously belonging to Mexico, and which remain for the future within the limits of the United States, as defined by the present treaty, shall be free to continue where they now reside, or to remove at any time to the Mexican Republic, retaining the property which they possess in the said territories, or disposing thereof, and removing the proceeds wherever they please, without their being subjected, on this account, to any contribution, tax, or charge whatever.

Those who shall prefer to remain in the said territories may either retain the title and rights of Mexican citizens, or acquire those of citizens of the United States. But they shall be under the obligation to make their election within one year from the date of the exchange of ratifications of this treaty; and those who shall remain in the said territories after the expiration of that year, without having declared their intention to retain the character of Mexicans, shall be considered to have elected to become citizens of the United States.

In the said territories, property of every kind, now belonging to Mexicans not established there, shall be inviolably respected. The present owners, the heirs of these, and all Mexicans who may hereafter acquire said property by contract, shall enjoy with respect to it guarantees equally ample as if the same belonged to citizens of the United States.

※PROLOGUE※

Tierra Amarilla, New Mexico

Manuelito leapt from the school bus to the dirt road and in two strides topped the porch to the weaving store. He pulled open the screen door, not hearing it slam shut until he was through the showroom and into the kitchen that doubled as his mother's office. Panting, he dropped the backpack beside her desk and waited as she spoke on her mobile phone.

She glanced at him, her dark eyes unfocused, her mind on the call. She spoke quickly, fiddling with a pencil, then said, "Yes," followed by a pause, then said, "No. That's impossible. All of our items are handmade on a loom. We are unable to fill an order like that in such a short time." Her eyes moved to him again, still unfocused.

Manuelito pointed toward the distance, the foothills nearby.

She nodded approval, knowing that he was going to see his grandfather, El Viejo.

Manuelito went to the sink and drew a glass of water, gulping it down. He sighed, clunked the heavy bottomed glass on the chipped Mexican tile counter, and wiping his chin, turned and ran out the door.

The wind tried to slow him, but it was no match.

Viejo says that when the wind stops, summer has come. Viejo laughs his squeaky laugh, coughs and spits, and with a thick finger wipes the corner of his wrinkled mouth.

Manuelito stiff-armed the chalky hulk of a rusted and weed-choked Chevrolet, its hood open like the groaning maw of a long-dead beast. He stepped on the sagging bottom strand of a barbed wire fence, lifted the upper strand, ducked through, and sprinted across the soft, moist earth of the pasture, disturbing a small flock of Canadian geese that honked noisily.

He leapt a cattle guard and sprinted up the rutted road to where Viejo was tending the flock in the tall spring grass. Viejo was moving the sheep to the higher mountain pastures where the snow had melted and the grass was fresh and green. Manuelito slowed, his heart thumping, and yanked a long stem of the knee-high grass, biting off the tender bottom. The wind softened and the aspens flickered. Stopping, he turned to face the breeze and listened intently over his own heavy breath for the bleating of the sheep.

Manuelito crested a rise and saw sheep tracks and tufts of chewed grass. He looked for the hoof prints of Viejo's appaloosa and listened again for the lambs and the clanking of the lead ram's bell. Only the wind swished through the trees.

Climbing another rise, he saw the sheep in the deep grass, partially hidden in the cool shadows of the aspen trees. The sheep lifted their heads, almost in unison, taking note of him. Some bleated and moved away, the lambs prancing behind. A few sheep had wandered through a section of cut fence where the barbed wire strands curled back stiffly. He crossed a shallow wash and stood at the fence line in the shadows of the trees. A chill rippled through his young body.

Viejo's appaloosa grazed under a tall ponderosa, the reins dragging on the ground. *Viejo* was getting sloppy, Manuelito thought. As he approached the horse, Appy tried to move away, but stepped on a rein that tugged the bit and made him stop.

"Whoa," Manuelito said, grabbing the stirrup of the weathered black saddle with his right hand and reaching for the loose reins with his left. Holding the reins, he jumped to put his left foot in the stirrup, grabbed the saddle horn, and pulled himself up and onto the creaky saddle. He clicked his tongue and gave Appy a tap with his boot heels.

As the horse moved, Manuelito glimpsed a boot and then a pant leg in the tall grass. Manuelito swallowed hard as his heart pounded, fearing what he suspected.

"*Viejo! Viejo!*" he called out, his throat tight. He slipped from the saddle and stumbled slightly as he hit ground and stopped short.

El Viejo lay face down in the shadows, not moving.

Manuelito trembled as warm tears dribbled down his cheeks. He dropped to his knees beside the old man's body, touching Viejo's back through the faded blue work shirt. His fingers stopped at the large splotch of dried and dark red blood that had saturated the cloth and was crusted at the edges. Viejo's lifeless body was cool to the touch. One arm was splayed, the hand gripping the old, western-styled Colt six-shooter that Viejo always carried to keep away the coyotes. Manuelito sank to his knees and sobbed.

※1※

Santa Fe, New Mexico

The cold that swept into northern New Mexico late that winter was followed by heavy spring snows that broke tree branches, snapped power lines, and left the back roads muddy. But the trees budded, like they always did, and the grass greened around the base of the bronze statue of Pueblo women now lighted by the bright morning sun that greeted visitors to the New Mexico state capitol.

Luke Jackson shifted the shoulder strap of his canvas briefcase where he carried the tools of his trade: a pocket full of his roller-ball pens, a half-dozen of the narrow, spiral-bound reporter's notebooks, and a week's worth of outdated press releases as he hustled along the wet, tree-lined walkway to the heavy brass doors of the New Mexico state capitol.

Jackson nodded to the doorman, who opened one of the doors, like he did for all visitors, and crossed the marbled lobby, skirting a crowd bunched at the elevator that would take them to the upper floor meeting rooms and offices of the legislators and the governor. He hurried down the curving hallway of offices smelling of freshly brewed coffee and milling with people.

He pushed open a door marked with a placard that read PRESS and entered a room of cubicles created by gray fabric-covered dividers. He plopped his briefcase on his padded stenographer's chair and shed his coat. He picked up his coffee cup and rinsed it in the hallway drinking fountain before heading to the capitol's cafeteria.

Lobbyists huddled in dim corners along the curving hallway, talking in subdued, but intense tones on their cellular telephones outside the capitol's cramped message center.

In the cafeteria, Jackson flicked the spigot of a tall stainless-steel coffee pot and filled his mug.

"It's all over but the crying."

Jackson turned to the voice, which belonged to Frank Norton, a lobbyist and a big man with a bushy red handlebar mustache and thick, riotous red eyebrows.

"How'd you do this session?" Jackson asked.

"Win some. Lose some," Norton said with a cynical chuckle. "I get paid, either way."

"So do I," Jackson said as he blew across his steaming hot coffee to cool it.

Back at his desk in the press room, Jackson listened to his phone messages. After jotting down some call-back numbers, he drew a deep breath and called his editor. Her name was Judy Shores and he told her to expect a lengthy recap of the good, the bad, and the ugly of the legislative session. "It's all over but the crying," he said, borrowing Norton's line.

"What does that mean?" Shores asked.

"Nothing really," Jackson said with a sigh, "Talk to you later." He clicked off and sipped his coffee. After a moment, he rose and stepped into the next cubicle, asking, "Got today's paper?"

His eyes glued to his laptop, Terry Collins of the *Albuquerque Journal* lifted his thumb over his shoulder and to a pile of newspapers. "It's on the top."

Jackson grabbed a copy, scanned the front page, then opened the section to the newspaper's inside page dedicated to legislative news.

"I won three times last night," Collins said.

Jackson swallowed anxiously, fearing he'd been scooped, then looked curiously at Collins' computer screen where Collins was playing computer solitaire.

Jackson sighed. "You're ready for the big leagues," Jackson said as he scanned the headlines of the legislative page. One read, "Three Strikes and You're Out, Still In." Another proclaimed, "Power of the Pump: Gas Prices Go Up." A third was, "Not Gay Over Rights." He scanned the opinion page and a commentary on the relative intelligence of the legislators. Jackson smiled, refolded the paper, and tossed it back on the pile.

"Shit!" A hand slammed the desk in the next cubical. Jackson turned to see Alex Martinez, the Associated Press reporter, his dark eyes glaring. "I was here till goddamn one o'clock this morning babysitting these goddamn idiots and all the bastards in the bureau want is a goddamn list of bills. It's goddamn bullshit."

"So, tell me how you *really* feel," Jackson said with a chuckle.

"Fuck you," Martinez muttered.

"So what *did* our duly elected representatives do here until one o'clock this morning?"

"The Republicans in the senate filibustered the gay rights bill. Finally everyone got tired so they recessed. It's dead." Martinez pulled off his glasses and rubbed his eyes. "And I was here for the whole thing."

"They probably all got thirsty and wanted a drink."

"There's a press conference in five minutes," Martinez said.

"It's too early for that," Jackson said. "I haven't had my coffee yet."

Martinez shook his head slowly.

"Who called it?" Jackson asked.

"Vincent Mallory. The lawyer. It's about illegal campaign contributions."

"No end of fun," Jackson said, sipping from his coffee. He slipped a fresh notebook in his sport coat pocket, checked for his pen, and walked with Martinez down the stairs to Mallory's office in the capitol's basement. Television crews were already setting up. Collins, along with Phil Sandusky of the *Albuquerque Tribune* and Donna Brock of the Associated Press waited, looking bored and anxious.

"While you guys are setting up, I'll distribute some documents," Mallory said. "There should be enough for everyone." Mallory's hands trembled as he handed out the stapled press releases.

Sandusky rolled his eyes at Jackson as Mallory sat at his desk and straightened his tie.

"Ready?" Mallory asked, scanning the assembled press.

The television crews nodded and clicked on the glaring camera lights.

Mallory cleared his throat. "You are all aware of the Speaker's Fund. It's the name given to the campaign contributions given to House Speaker Johnny Socorro during the annual legislative session. Socorro, being a Democrat, has used the money to back specific candidates for the Legislature, all of whom are Democrats, of course. However, Socorro hasn't filed campaign expense reports detailing the distribution and use of those funds. That's a clear violation of state campaign reporting law."

Pink faced, Mallory glanced at the reporters then brushed sweat from his curled upper lip.

"You're accusing the speaker of the house of violating the state's campaign contributions law?" Brock asked.

Mallory swallowed and nodded. "Go to the Secretary of State's office. Look for yourself. There are no expense reports. Socorro has never filed reports as to where the money goes. For all anyone knows, he may be keeping the money for himself."

"Do you think he's doing that?" Brock asked.

Mallory shifted. Sweat gleamed on his high forehead. "I can't answer that. No one knows. Socorro doesn't file the reports."

"Your campaign finance reform bill is dead, right?" Collins asked, scratching his beard.

"For the past four years," Mallory replied, "my attempts to bring openness and accountability to the financing of political campaigns in this state have passed the Senate, but died in the House. Why? Certain people do not want the public to know who finances the political campaigns in this state."

"Like House Speaker Socorro?" Sandusky asked.

Mallory nodded. "The campaign financing documents are supposed to be filed at the Secretary of State's office. But they don't exist."

"Why are you talking about this now, on the last day of the legislative session?" Jackson asked.

"So maybe you people in the news media will write about it."

"We have," Sandusky said. "Socorro keeps getting re-elected."

Mallory just stared.

"Is this your last session?" Brock asked.

Mallory scowled and folded his arms across his chest. "Probably. I have more productive ways to spend my time than trying to bring openness and honesty to the political process in this state."

The room was silent. The reporters looked at Mallory, then at each other.

"If there are no more questions, that's all I have," Mallory said. He scanned the reporters, then nodded and stood. "Thank you for coming."

Jackson hurried onto the open floor of the House chamber floor where legislators chatted during a short recess. He spotted Socorro, a short and stocky man with broad shoulders and thick, graying hair, in the midst of an animated conversation with two other legislators. Jackson paused several steps away and waved to get Socorro's attention. Socorro stopped mid-sentence, turned and frowned. Jackson stepped forward.

"Vince Mallory just had a press conference about your lack of campaign contribution reports," Jackson blurted, showing Socorro the news release. "He handed these out."

Socorro scanned the sheets of paper, then looked up, his eyes narrowing.

"Mallory says you violate campaign reporting laws."

"Goddam it!" Socorro wadded the paper into a ball and threw it on the floor, then turned and stomped away. After several steps, he stopped, wheeled, and marched back. Socorro grabbed Jackson's coat lapels and jerked Jackson's face close to his own. "You tell that son-of-a-bitch...I... have...never... ever...broken...campaign...laws."

Jackson felt Socorro's hot breath in his face. Socorro shoved Jackson back and released his lapels. Stunned, Jackson stared wide-eyed at Socorro, then lifted his pen to the pad to jot down the comment, but his hand was shaking so badly he couldn't write. Jackson opened his mouth to speak as Socorro waved a finger an inch from Jackson's nose. "You tell Mallory he'd better watch out. He'd better be careful what he says." Socorro whirled again and stomped away.

Jackson was still shaking back at the pressroom where he threw his pen and notepad against the wall of his fabric-covered cubical. "Shit. Shit. Shit," he sputtered. His head throbbed, his back ached. He massaged his temples, then touched his stomach where the coffee burned like acid. He took a few deep breaths and slowly exhaled. The legislative session was almost over. He went outside for some fresh air.

※2※

Ojo Caliente

Warmth rose from Jackson's feet to his knees as he stepped into the sulfur-scented mineral pool at the Ojo Caliente hot springs. His skin tingled as he sank into the warm water. He took comfort in the Spanish word *ojo*, which meant eye, and in this instance was the eye of God. Ojo caliente was "hot eye" and the term for a hot spring, since the healing waters of this ancient spring was considered a blessing from God. But for the moment, Jackson didn't think about that. He only wanted relief from the legislative session that had ended just days earlier.

He mindlessly paddled about in the warm pool like a child. The rock walls were warm and slick. Resting against one, he closed his eyes and listened to the confusion of voices, words, and numbers of the legislative session that lingered inside his head, like the remnants of disturbing dream. In his mind's eye, faces bobbed in and out of focus. *Go away*, he thought, *just go away*.

Half an hour later he emerged, his body pink and dripping wet, sweat stinging his eyes. Other mineral pools beckoned, each holding the promise of a cure, but he would try them later. He cooled in the spring air as he pattered barefoot across the concrete, dressed only in his swim trunks, a towel draped around his neck, to the rock drinking fountain of lithium water. He filled a paper cup and drank. Lithium was nature's Prozac, they claimed. The water was warm and tasted strange. He sloshed it around in his mouth and swallowed.

Sunbathers were sprawled on padded wooden chaise lounges arranged around another shallow pool. Beyond the spa's perimeter fence, the faded reds and pink of the sandstone cliffs and pinon-studded hills surrounded the pools as if the steaming waters were hidden treasures amidst the protective earth. The sparsely treed hills rose to the piñon and bristle cone pine trees that spread like green skirts along the base of the distant snowy peaks of the Sangre de Cristo Mountains outlined sharply against the deep blue sky.

Jackson drank a couple more cups of lithium water as a breeze kicked up, chilling his skin. He toweled his hair, checked his watch, and went to the large brown building where he was scheduled for a massage. Tying the towel around his waist, he walked down the hall to a door marked "12." He knocked.

"You can come in," a woman's voice said.

He pushed it open.

Inside, a woman with thick, tawny hair and pale blue eyes looked at him from across the massage table. "Mr. Jackson?"

He nodded.

"I'm Ariel and I'll be your massage therapist for today." She was shoulder high to Jackson and wore a light blue cotton polo shirt monogrammed with Ojo Caliente. "Undress and make yourself comfortable on a massage table, face down, and cover yourself with that towel. I'll be back in a minute." She disappeared behind a door and closed it.

He stepped out of his swim suit, hung it on a peg, and climbed on the table, lying face down, as instructed, with a white cotton towel covering his behind.

Ariel returned, and after adjusting the towel, slipped a disc into a player and coated her hands with lotion. Soft flute and harp music drifted over a background of crashing waves. She started on his cramped neck and tight shoulder muscles. Jackson's mind quickly dulled.

"Your shoulders and upper back muscles are knotted," Ariel said.

He let his arms hang from the sides of the table as she kneaded the torqued tissue between his shoulder blades. There was a place—it was the trapezius muscle, because he'd looked it up—that always hurt. On deadline, it felt like he'd been stabbed in that spot. After deadline and a couple of drinks, the pain melted away. Ariel quickly found the spot and using her fingers, pushed away the tension, easing his pain. "I just finished two months at the state legislature," he said, somewhat defensively. "I'm a journalist."

"I don't follow the news much," she said, gently working a knuckle into his knotted muscle tissue.

A jolt of pain shot across Jackson's back and up to the base of his skull. He flinched.

"Was that too hard?" she asked.

"I guess," he groaned.

"Anyway, life's too short to worry about all the problems of the world," she said with a breathy sigh.

Lifting his forearm onto his lower back, she worked her fingers under his upraised shoulder blade. She found more knotted muscle and pushed.

Again, he felt a stab of pain in his back and flinched. "Ouch!"

She pulled back. "I'm sorry."

"It's all right," he wheezed.

"It's a common hiding place for tension." She worked the spot more gently. "The news is always so upsetting. The same awful things over and over again."

Jackson's stomach gurgled. He was too exhausted to respond, but privately, he agreed. Year after year, the stories were same; only the names changed. Thousands of pieces of legislation were introduced each year, each meant to fix something for someone, rightly or wrongly, the bill sponsors claiming they wanted to make society better or safer or to make someone pay more taxes or less taxes. More often than not, the bills that were introduced would make someone money. Some of the laws worked, but most had little or no effect on the vast majority of people who went about their daily lives, saying and doing what they always had.

"Making a better world begins with each person," Ariel continued. "People should look inward, not outward."

Jackson said nothing. He hated sentences that began with "people should." The word should had little meaning for him. People either did things or didn't do things. Most often, the reasons why were forgotten along the way, and in the end just didn't matter.

Ariel worked on his hamstring, pressing both thumbs deep and working them down to the back of his knee. She found places that Jackson didn't know hurt. She thumbed his calf muscles and then his Achilles tendon as jolts of pain ran up and down his leg. His feet had felt like dead clumps, but she brought them back to life and left them throbbing with life.

"You can turn over now."

Jackson rolled, careful to cover himself.

Ariel's pale blue eyes seemed very serious. Her long, thick hair had a natural wave and was tied loosely behind her head. She finished by standing at the head of the table and massaging his temples. She said he could lay there for a while.

He did. His body felt like putty.

She busied herself folding and stacking towels, then paused at the door. "I'll let you get dressed."

After a few minutes, Jackson sat upright slowly and dangled his legs from the side of the table. He felt like he was floating and for a moment was disoriented.

§

It was called "veggie loaf" and was the spa restaurant's special that evening, served with brown rice, steamed carrots and arugula salad doused with a red wine vinaigrette. Jackson ate slowly, the first meal he had taken time to enjoy in months. He glanced around the restaurant, gazing absentmindedly at the white-plastered walls, the varnished *vigas* overhead, the checkered table cloths, and the hand-made stoneware. He sipped herbal iced tea with a sprig of fresh mint.

Two elderly women and two middle-aged couples, one speaking German, were in the restaurant. Jackson hoped that Ariel would show somehow, even though he hadn't bothered to invite her, and watched the door as diners came and went. A woman's touch, he thought. That too, had been months. *You need to treat yourself better*, he told himself. *But you've been there before. You've done that. And it can hurt.* Still, he thought about Ariel.

After dinner he walked in the fading light along the graveled drive to his room in the row of casitas. He was achingly tired. He inhaled deeply and studied the evening star near a crescent moon—a picture perfect moment. Cars passed on the nearby highway. At the door to his casita, he paused, then turned to his compact Toyota pickup truck and climbed in.

The dirt road from the spa ended at the paved highway. Jackson's truck bounced onto it, and after a quarter mile, he turned into a gas station where a neon Coors sign glowed. Moths swarmed around a bare light bulb below a metal lamp shade, their shadows flickering on oil-stained concrete. Gasoline was being pumped into a battered four-wheel drive Ford pickup with large, knobby off-road tires and an open can of Budweiser beer balanced on the dash. The driver leaned against the truck with one hand, his other grasping the nozzle, and with glistening dark eyes, stared at Jackson from under a sweat-stained cowboy hat.

Inside the store, the worn, wooden floor creaked as Jackson walked past shelves of canned goods, boxes of dry foods, and several tall coolers where he grabbed a six-pack of Corona bottles. He asked the man at the counter for a lime. The man nodded to a boy with large eyes and cropped black hair, who slipped casually off a stool and disappeared into the back. Jackson pointed to a pint of José Cuervo gold on the shelf behind the counter.

Outside, the truck engine revved and the rear tires truck squealed. The man at the cash register shook his head in disgust and punched the keys. "Nine sixty one," he said.

Jackson handed the man a ten dollar bill and accepted the change.

Back in his casita, Jackson squeezed a wedge of lime juice into his beer and watched it sink and swirl. He stuffed the wedge into the top of the bottle, watched it float, and took long, gulping swallows. He held the bottle on his stomach and used the remote control to turn on the television, leaving the sound off. Muted characters talked and moved, then were replaced by advertisements for cars, laxatives, and beer. Millions of people, night after night, watched this stuff, he thought. Now he was one of them. The logo design on the Corona bottle was more interesting. He scratched at it with a thumbnail, but it didn't come off.

§

Sunlight angled through the venetian blinds, glinting off the empty beer bottles on the nightstand. Jackson rolled over and gazed at the flecks of dust floating in the air. At first he did not remember, but then he recalled his dreams. The first had been of his ex-wife. She'd been with a country music star, a man who lived in Taos in a sprawling adobe house filled with western gear. The star had bought her a new Toyota Land Cruiser to replace her old one.

Jackson then dreamt someone was attacking him with a hammer. He'd picked up a hammer of his own and swung back, fending off the attacker. Dreams were supposed to be messages from the unconscious. *What the hell did this one mean?* He didn't want to think about it, so he crawled out of bed, feeling achy and stiff, and checked his watch: 8:47. The morning was well along.

The outdoor mineral pools were already occupied as he walked to the spa restaurant for breakfast. He was late and the dining room was nearly empty, save for one couple drinking coffee as the kitchen help noisily washed dishes. When no waitress appeared, he went to the kitchen doorway where a plump woman in a white uniform, her hair slung in a net and her hands deep in foamy wash water. "We're closing soon," she said. She paused to look at him questioningly. His stomach gurgled. He needed coffee.

"What would you like?" said a soft voice behind him. It belonged to Ariel, the massage therapist.

Jackson smiled. "If you're closed...."

Ariel shook her head and again asked, "What would you like?" She spoke as if she owned the place. She motioned him to a table where she placed a menu.

"You work here as well?" he asked.

She shrugged.

Jackson glanced at the table, then asked, "What do you recommend?"

He accepted her suggestion and was soon digging into a bowl of vanilla yogurt topped with bananas, blueberries, almonds, and walnuts. He paused only to sip black coffee from a handmade ceramic cup. He tried to think of what he would do that day, but came up empty. He gazed out the restaurant windows where the piñon pines dotted the gritty red hills. Outside a tractor started up noisily and chugged down the spa's dirt road, the sound fading as he ate.

§

An hour later Jackson sped down the aging two-lane blacktop road, his sunglasses softening the glare of the morning sun from between clouds floating in the blue above snow-capped mountains. The scent of fields freshly spread with manure swirled inside his partly open windows. To his right, a billboard depicted a bull elk and a pink-green trout leaping from opposite corners and proclaimed a bounty of hunting and fishing in northern New Mexico. Jackson imagined himself by a rushing stream, a fly rod in his hand, the line floating out and over tumbling stream waters, and then the sudden tug of a trout on the line. He slowed and veered impulsively onto another narrow two-lane road that dropped down a hillside and into El Valle, a village of adobe and wood-frame houses, most with corrugated metal roofs and fronted by an occasional aging car or truck sitting on concrete blocks.

He stopped in front of a small building marked with a modest sign telling him this was La Tienda Lana, the wool store. There were no other cars. The place looked deserted. He set the brake, and as he stepped onto the broad wooden porch, he peered into the darkened store. When he tried the door handle, it gave way and a bell tinkled above him.

Inside, the store was silent. Woven blankets, *serapes,* and sweaters hung from round chrome racks. Along the walls, white shelves were stacked with more folded wool goods. Stacks of rugs covered the hardwood floor. Skeins of naturally dyed wool hung from wall pegs. He caressed the hanging wool, lifted it to his nose and inhaled the natural scent. He ran a hand between the piled rugs and flipped up a corner.

"We're closed."

Jackson turned. He'd heard that once already today. A plump woman with bulbous cheeks and black hair tied in a long braid leaned forward with her arms spread wide and her hands planted on the counter. The skin around her left eye was scarred and the eye stared blindly straight ahead. The right eye moved quickly, oddly searching him.

"No one's here," she said.

"Can I look for a few minutes?"

"We're closed," she said again, turning to the window. "Funeral today. A big one." She stared out the window and sighed.

He went to a pile of smaller rugs, pulled one out and held it up. Red, brown, gray and black. He draped it over his forearm then picked up another. $175 was penciled on a small white tag. He carried them both to the counter. "I found something I like." Jackson felt for his checkbook in his jacket pocket, unzipped it, and pulled the check book out.

She held up her hand. "You can't buy it today. I can't take the money. Come back tomorrow."

The woman's good eye stared at him. She was serious.

"I don't want to come back tomorrow," he said.

She looked at him and said nothing.

Jackson mulled his options. There were none. "So who died?"

"*El viejo,*" she said softly.

"*El viejo*?" he asked.

She nodded. “He took care of the sheep for the village. *El era un padre por todo el mundo.*” She turned her head slowly from side to side, a pained look on her face. “Somebody shot him.”

“Really?”

“They found him with his sheep. *El nieto* found him. Manuelito. *Probrecito*,” she said, mumbling.

Jackson had heard nothing about an old shepherd being shot to death. “When did this happen?”

“A few days ago. *Tres dias, pienso*.” Outside, church bells began to peel. “They’re coming. *La procesión*. They’re going to bury *El Viejo* today. Come back tomorrow. We’re shearing the sheep then. Everyone will be here.” She came around the counter and touched his arm. “You go. I lock up now.”

Jackson stepped outside and onto the porch as she closed the door behind him, turned the lock with a click, and pulled down a shade with a sign that read, CLOSED. Jackson squinted down the road toward a procession of twenty or so people moving slowly toward him, shuffling, stepping solemnly. Struck by their gravity, he waited. Furrowed and serious, the faces were shadowed under wool scarves, well-worn baseball caps, and cowboy hats. Hands were folded, eyes downcast. The two dozen people followed the large doll figure atop a pole of the saint, Our Lady of Guadalupe, her serenity frozen on a pink, porcelain face, her body surrounded by a yellow aura, her white hands opened. The figure bobbed and wove through the air.

Men in dark coats carried a casket on their shoulders. They were trailed by a boy leading a saddled Appaloosa without a rider. The white handkerchiefs of the women dabbed at eyes hidden behind black lace. Jackson was tempted to fall into the entourage and be drawn along in its wake. But he would be an interloper, uninvited. He watched the assembly follow the curve of the road to the plastered adobe church, climb the steps, and disappear into the darkened doorway.

※3※

Tierra Amarilla

Jackson awoke early the next morning. He got up, took a hot shower, dressed, and headed to the spa's restaurant for breakfast. Several cups of strong, black coffee, along with a breakfast burrito of scrambled eggs and beans, topped with green chili sauce, filled his stomach as he tossed his canvas duffel bag in the back of his truck and slammed the camper shell shut.

An overnight frost had painted an elaborate design across the windshield. He turned on the defroster and the windshield wipers, then checked his camera bag: six rolls of film. He had learned from the woman at the wool shop that there'd be a sheep shearing that day, so he'd called his editor and gotten approval to write a story and take photos of this annual springtime ritual among the sheep ranchers of rural northern New Mexico.

It also meant he could spend another night at the spa where he hoped to see Ariel. Late in the afternoon the day before, he had asked for her at the massage building. But it was not to be. He was told she had that night off.

With a selection of good photos, a story about the traditional Spring sheep shearing by the wool growers and weavers of the north would make a good feature story package. His editor had loved the idea because it was a glimpse into a lifestyle now lost to most of America.

When Jackson arrived, pickup trucks lined the road near the wool store. He checked his watch. It was just past eight o'clock. Jackson locked his truck, slipped his camera bag over his shoulder, and checked for his notebook, pens, and his recorder. He was set.

The bell jingled overhead as he opened the door to the wool shop. The scent of coffee and cooking filled the air. The store lights were on, but no one was at the sales counter. The early morning sun shined brightly into the shop's back room filled with a half a dozen looms.

Voices and laughter floated from a large kitchen in the back. When Jackson appeared in the doorway, several elderly men sat at the kitchen table, hands cupped around coffee mugs. A couple of women in jeans and head scarves stood at a stove. A carton of eggs was open on the counter. He smelled frying chorizo. One woman warmed a tortilla on a griddle, flipping it delicately with her fingers. They turned and fell silent as Jackson paused, then they slowly returned to what they were saying and doing, without acknowledging him.

A slender woman with dark hair pulled into a tight ponytail sat at the kitchen table and talked on a cell phone. She raised a finger signaling for him to wait. "*Si, si, bueno* bye," she said, then hung up and turned to him. "Can I help you?"

Jackson stammered that he was a journalist with *The New Mexican* newspaper in Santa Fe and had stopped by the store the day before.

"We are closed for my father's funeral," she replied before he could explain what he wanted to do. She was clearly uninterested in him and his reason for being there. She stared, waiting for him to leave, then cleared her throat to emphasize her point.

Jackson stepped forward, extended an arm, and handed her his business card.

She looked at it briefly.

"I'm here to do a story on sheep shearing," he said, stating it as a matter of fact.

After a moment's hesitation, she nodded. It was a gesture that Jackson took as acceptance of him and his assignment.

"I'm Antonia Aguilar," she said with authority. She pulled a business card of her own from a bowl on her desk and handed it to him. It said she was the director of *El Cooperativo del Valle* and general manager of La Tienda Lana. "You work for *The New Mexican* newspaper in Santa Fe?"

"I do."

"I recognize the name. You've written some articles about the people in the north."

Jackson nodded.

"They were good," she said.

"Thanks. I was told there'll be shearing of sheep today. I was hoping to do a story and take some photos."

She nodded agreeably. "We need all the publicity we can get." She handed him a brochure. "We're a wool-growing cooperative. We consolidated our flocks and graze them on traditional community lands, the old Spanish land grant." She paused.

Jackson knew the back story, which was part of the reason he'd come to do the story. Deep social and political tensions swirled around the historic land grants, which had not always been peaceful. Beginning in the late 1500s, the Spanish ruled Mexico, which included most of the American Southwest including all of Nevada and California. The Spanish handed out land grants both to individuals and communities. Later the Mexican government did the same thing.

The free land was meant to spur people to settle what was originally Spain's and then Mexico's northern territories. But records of who owned what and where were lost over time, much of it burned or lost back in 1680 during the Pueblo Revolt when the native communities along the Rio Grande rose up to drive the Spanish out.

The Tierra Amarilla grant was created in 1832, some two hundred years later, by the Mexican government and deeded to a man named Manuel Martinez and other settlers in the area of what is now known as Abiquiu. The grant encompassed much more than what was currently known as Tierra Amarilla County, which meant the Yellow Land. But the land grant had not been the gift that many assumed. The grantees were repeatedly attacked during deadly raids by the local native tribes, including the Utes, Navajo, and the Jicarilla Apaches until the early 1860s.

That's went the U.S. Congress, lobbied heavily by Anglo land speculators, pronounced the land grant was a private, not a community land grant, citing some mistranslated and obscure documents. Despite the lack of an official title, which would have required an official survey, the heirs of the original grantee, Manuel Martinez, began to sell parcels to speculators. Among the buyers was the influential lawyer, Thomas B. Catron of Santa Fe. Then in 1880, with title in hand, Catron sold some of the former grant land to the Denver and Rio Grande Railway so it could build a rail line north to Chama, thereby establishing a precedent of his ownership.

Within a couple of years, Catron had consolidated all of land grant deeds, but the deeds excluded the original villages and the affiliated fields. Aware that they were losing their lands after seventy years' passing, the descendants of the original grantees eventually petitioned the courts in 1950 to reclaim the communal land. Their requests were denied.

The lingering resentment and smoldering hostility still burned among the community, which was why Jackson wanted badly to be at the camp. His stories would add a new chapter to the region's history.

"This is the last shearing of the spring," Aguilar said.

"Pictures are all right, I assume?"

"Of course. Have you eaten?"

"As a matter of fact, I have," Jackson said.

Antonia ignored him and called out, "Maria! *Tenemos comida por el señor*?"

"*Si. Hay mucho*," Maria said with a laugh. Jackson went to the counter and watched as Maria used a large wooden spoon to load a mix of fried potatoes, beans, and chorizo onto a slightly scorched tortilla that she folded then covered with steaming red chili sauce.

Jackson smiled and nodded appreciatively as he inhaled the aromas. Taking a chair beside Antonia's desk, he ate slowly with the plate on his lap.

"You should write about my father," Antonia said. She leaned close and whispered, "*Viejo* was murdered."

Jackson chewed slowly as the chili warmed his stomach. "A woman yesterday told me about that."

"No one cares about us or what happens up here. We're just a bunch *Mejicanos*."

Jackson took another bite. "Have you gone to the police?"

She laughed bitterly. "The sheriff? They won't do nothin'."

"The sheriff needs to handle this sort of thing."

"They say they're investigating, but they're not."

"It wasn't an accident?"

"Accidentally shot in the back?" she asked, then glared and waved her hand dismissively.

The story he had in mind earlier now pivoted. A feature story and photos on the wool cooperative would be an easy one, a feel-good piece about the pastoral life in rural northern New Mexico. But an old shepherd murdered? He doubted his editors would be interested unless there was an investigation. He'd have to contact law enforcement for that. Without them, it was just speculation and accusations. Still, he knew he had to look into it.

"Good point," Jackson said.

Antonia nodded.

The burrito and red chili smoldered in Jackson's stomach as Antonia lead him back out through the weaving room, where she paused and motioned to the looms. They were owned by the *cooperativo* and were leased to the weavers, she explained. The blankets, shawls, rugs, jackets, and other items were sold in the store on consignment, which kept the overhead to a minimum. Weaver's expenses, including the wool, were deducted from the sales. Jackson jotted notes as Antonia spoke.

Outside, sheep bleated loudly from inside the gray and warped wooden rails of the corrals. Jackson checked the camera's exposure as sheep were yanked from the pen by their back legs. Two men flipped each one roughly to its side and held it down, one tugging the front legs, the other the rear. Electric shears shaved the matted, dirty wool from the sheep in thick slabs that were gathered by the armful and carried to a corrugated metal shed to be washed and dyed.

Once shorn, each sheep struggled to its feet, bleated, and shook itself, strangely free of its warm winter coats. A young boy whacked each with a stick and sent it scurrying into the adjacent open field.

The shearer had thick arms and wide hands, and stood upright to relieve his back. He wiped sweat from his forehead with the back of his leather glove and exhaled his hot breath into the cold air. He motioned for another animal.

Jackson captured the action from various angles. After dozens of shots and about a dozen sheep, the trio took a break. Jackson took out his notebook and introduced himself.

"Where'd you learn to shear like that?" he asked the shearer.

The man sighed, looked off into the distance, then back at Jackson. "I don't want to be in your story."

Jackson scowled. "I've been taking pictures of you all this time. It's a little late."

"I don't want my picture in the paper." The man wiped his face with a sleeve and narrowed his eyes.

"I'm doing a story for the Santa Fe newspaper. I've cleared it with Antonia."

The man shook his head. "I'm not Antonia." He turned to one of the others. "Is there any coffee?" One with an old and stained gray cowboy hat nodded and went toward the house.

"It's a little hard to take pictures of a sheep shearing with no shearer."

The man shook his head. "No pictures. No names."

Jackson stared down at his camera, then squinted at the shearer. He was backlit by the sun. "You should have said something earlier."

"Interview him," the shearer said, pointing to his companion. "He likes that kind of thing."

The one with the cowboy hat returned, holding three coffee cups. He handed out the cups, then nodded cautiously at Jackson.

"Trini Gonzales," he said extending a limp hand, as was the custom. Jackson shook it gently. Gonzales had a deeply lined, leathery face, and dark, mischievous eyes.

The three men squatted to rest and sipped from the cups. Jackson crouched as well, resting on one knee.

"So, you doin' a story?" Gonzales asked.

Jackson nodded. "Yeah. Your friend here says he doesn't want to be in it."

Gonzales was a lithe, wiry man, and pushed his sweat stained hat back on his head with his thumb. "Sixto's already been famous." Gonzales chuckled. "Didn't like it much."

Sixto glowered.

Trini shook his head.

Jackson turned to Sixto, who nodded.

"Sixto Hernandez," he said with a pained smile that fell away instantly. He dropped his eyes to the ground and sipped from his coffee. Hernandez was the biggest, well built, and offered a pained look.

Jackson turned to Gonzales. "Do you mind if I take pictures of you?" Jackson asked.

Gonzales shrugged.

Jackson nodded, then asked, "So how long you been doing this?"

Gonzales laughed. "How long? Ever since I can remember. You just grow up with this. We all did."

"Are you a sheep rancher?"

Gonzales shook his head no. "Hunting guide. I only come 'round when there's a party." He laughed.

"Do you have any sheep of your own?" Jackson asked.

Gonzales stared at Jackson and nodded slowly. He glanced at the others, then took a last swallow of his coffee before tossing the dregs to the dirt. Without a word, he pulled on his tan leather gloves and picked up the shears.

Hernandez grabbed another sheep, and flipped it on its side as Gonzales began to shear.

Jackson stepped back, refocused and took another dozen shots.

After ten minutes, he turned to Antonia, who motioned to the nearby array of steaming metal tubs.

"Here is where we dye the wool," Antonia said.

Steam roiled into the cool air from the dark liquid.

"It's all natural dyes from the plants we gather in the mountains."

Two other women with thick skeins of spun wool looped on their arms eased it into the steaming tubs, filling the air with the scent of wet wool. The women smiled shyly as Jackson clicked off frames while they slowly fed the wool in the tubs.

"People have done this here for hundreds of years," Antonia said. "This is our way of life. We want to keep it this way."

"How is the store doing?" Jackson asked after taking more frames.

"We're still here," she said, with a shrug, then squinted. "It's the best answer can give." She looked around for a moment and spoke softly. "You need to know that no one here is getting paid for their work today. They believe what we're doing. It's important that this way of life is preserved."

※4※

Santa Fe

The long hot shower felt good, but he still ached. It was a quiet, gray day and the sky looked like it couldn't decide whether to rain or snow. The neighbor's dog barked loudly at a package delivery truck. His terrycloth bathrobe draped open, Jackson sat in his underwear at his kitchen table, sipped black coffee, and surveyed the disarray of his rented condominium.

You should be able to do better than this, he told himself. But he had all the room he needed, and in truth the condo was all he could afford. He longed for the freedom and independence of freelance writing, but with his child support payments every month, he feared the financial irregularity that came with independence. That's why he'd never left *The New Mexican.* He knew he'd be constantly on the hustle, spending more time pitching stories than writing them. And when he might sell a story, it often took months to get paid. The small, glossy magazines were the worst. Payment on publication, they said. But in fact, they fleeced a writer like himself. They collected money from their advertisers and kept it. Paying writers was an afterthought. Don't think about it, he told himself.

The sun broke through the clouds, bathing his cramped, back patio in sunlight.

After refilling his coffee cup, he listened to his phone messages. His ex-wife Margo had called. "We need to talk," she'd said. "Where have you been? Your child support is way overdue. Luna would like to see you, you know."

His stomach soured. The pain returned to his shoulder blade.

The next message was from Luna. "Daddy, I miss you. Where have you been?"

He dialed the number to Margo's real estate office.

The phone rang several times, then a hassled female voice said, "Can you hold, please?"

"Goddam it," Jackson muttered. Put on hold before he could get a word out. When the voice returned, he asked for Margo McNeil. She'd never given up her maiden name.

"She's not in."

He waited for her to say she would take a message, but she didn't. "Can you take a message?"

"She's showing a home. Do you want her cell number?"

"I have it." Jackson hung up, scrolled through his phone's list of calls, then dialed. She answered. "Margo. It's...."

"Can't talk now."

"I have some money."

She sighed. "Meet me at the Pink Adobe a few minutes before noon."

"The Pink. Sure."

She hung up.

§

At eleven-thirty, Jackson stopped at the private mail stop he used, not trusting the town's mail delivery. The manager, a retired army sergeant named Murray, had a ball point pen wedged between two stubby fingers. "Yeah, you got lots of mail." He disappeared into the back then came out with a thick wad of envelopes bound with a heavy rubber band. "Where you been?" He exhaled loudly from behind a clear plastic shield and scratched his buzz-cut head.

Jackson looked at him. "I was on the road for a story for a few days. Went north." He eyed the bundle. "There better be money in here."

"There is."

"You checked already, did you?"

Murray smiled. "Don't need to. I can smell it."

Jackson slipped the rubber band from around the bundle and sorted through it. Murray was right. There were some checks from the freelance assignment he's secured. He suddenly felt flush now that a few payments had come. Except for a couple of bills, he tossed the junk mail into the trash.

"You know it's illegal to go through people's mail," Jackson said.

"Use the post office, then," Murray said with a matter-of-face stare.

Jackson shook his head.

§

Jackson parked in the empty lot beside the capitol. His desk in the press room cubicle was cluttered with a dozen or so press releases. Jesus, those people just don't stop with this stuff, he thought. He lifted one from the governor's office. Gov. Jack Carrow had signed bills over the weekend, mostly budgetary stuff. The biggest bill was a supplemental spending bill that had millions in add-ons. This was the pork.

Carrow was a conservative Republican with an MBA and a law degree. He had campaigned on cutting the state budget, and routinely talked about budget issues for the television cameras using big colorful pie charts. After signing a state budget that included cuts and reductions in public spending, now that the session was over and the legislators and press were gone, Carrow had signed an innocuous bill called "supplemental" spending. Jackson read down the list of the special projects in it. None of it looked alarming, but he'd have to look at it more closely. That would be later.

§

He arrived at the Pink Adobe before Margo and took a seat at a window table near the smooth-plastered kiva fireplace in the Dragon Room. The clientele was a mixed crowd. Moneyed Texans, he guessed, and tinsel-towners, people who wore designer jeans and too much silver, and turquoise. A few lawyers in suits. Outside a dark green Range Rover stopped at the curb. Margo emerged. She said something to the man driving. From the doorway she scanned the restaurant like a shark, spotted him, and slipped out of her coat on the way to his table.

"I'm with a client," she said. "Someone I want you to meet, actually. Hope you don't mind."

"I'm sure he'll enjoy our conversation."

"Please don't. This guy is important to me."

"Big money, I suppose."

Her eyes narrowed. She dipped a hand into her purse, pulled out a compact and lipstick, and looked at herself quickly. Jackson pulled a check from his pocket, unfolded it, and handed it to her. "That should clear up what's past due and put me a month ahead."

"Where'd you get money like that?"

"I make money the old-fashioned way. I earn it."

Margo folded the check and slipped it into her wallet.

"When do I get to see Luna?"

"This weekend would be good. I'm going to LA."

"With your friend, Big Money?"

She nodded slightly. "You can pick Luna up Friday from school, at three. Don't be late. She'll be waiting." Margo turned to a figure standing in the doorway. He was tanned, square jawed, with a denim shirt studded with silver buttons, faded blue jeans, cowboy boots, and a silver and turquoise bolo tie. Margo waved, then rose to take his hand as he was seated. "Jim Fredrickson. This is Luke Jackson. I've told you about him."

Jackson casually reached across the table to shake the man's hand. Fredrickson's smile was confident, his brown eyes steady. He looked accustomed to getting what he wanted. He smiled warmly at Margo, then back at Jackson.

"Margo tells me you're a writer."

"Margo says a lot of things."

Margo shook her head disgustedly and looked down.

"You're not?" he asked.

"I'm a reporter with the local newspaper. *The New Mexican*."

"Jim's a film producer," Margo said.

"I admire writers," Fredrickson said. "They're the backbone of the film business. I've always wanted to write a book myself. Had a lot of experiences. Some amazing things go on in Hollywood."

"Hollywood stories sell well," Jackson said.

He fidgeted for a moment, debating whether to stay or go. But he just couldn't tamp down the roiling emotions that would not let him forgive Margo for their divorce. When she announced she wanted a divorce, Jackson felt like he'd been punched in the gut. Sure, he'd poured his heart and soul into his job, but he'd been faithful. He'd never strayed. As they say, he reminded himself, no good deed goes unpunished.

“I really hate to do this, but I need to run.” Jackson stood. “You two enjoy your lunch. See you Friday, Margo.”

Jackson turned and left.

※5※

Tierra Amarilla

Fields of fresh grass and the first crop of dark green alfalfa flanked the road north through the Rio Chama Valley. Leafy cottonwoods shimmered in the early summer breeze, shading collapsed adobe walls that hid cars and trucks mounted on cement blocks, their hoods open like the gaping mouths of dead beasts. The road snaked north, gradually climbing around rocky, layered cliffs of gray, yellow, and rust-red overlooking the muddy brown Rio Chama.

Jackson began to feel good, now that he was again headed north for what he hoped would be yet another exclusive story.

"If you want some news, be here," Antonia had said on the phone, then hung up. She had tweaked his imagination, tantalizing him with the prospect of getting a scoop. It could not have come at a better time, he thought, as he eagerly drove north.

The night before he had grown morose, worried about the future. The weather had not helped. He'd heard sirens late at night. An accident, maybe. Then came the thunder and lightning, followed by stillness. Finally the rain had fallen, softly at first, then in torrents. As quickly as it had come, the storm was gone, leaving the night air moist and cool and fresh.

Unable to sleep, Jackson had stared at a picture on his dresser drawers that had been taken when he and Margo were young and in love, standing on a rocky peak in Colorado's Sawatch Range. It had been a run-in-front. Jackson had balanced the camera on a rock and pushed the timer, giving him just enough time to scramble to her side. They were grinning in the sunlight, and for a moment they looked like two people he had never known.

Jackson had long since pushed the thoughts of the night from his mind as he found a place to park beside a television station's hulking white Chevy Suburban mounted with a video dish. It had pulled into the same gas station and general store he had visited just days earlier. Jackson listened as the same store clerk with the bad eye with whom he'd talked gave directions to a television reporter, while the cameraman sat on the porch smoking.

Fifteen minutes later, a dusty plume followed the small convoy of news media vehicles led by Jackson as he raced along the gravel road, braked as he approached a cattle guard, and turned up a rutted road flanked by pastures. He drove through an aspen grove and stopped where police and several federal vehicles were clustered near a fence gate. His pulse quickened.

Two tall posts, looking like cannibalized telephone poles, supported a thick crosspiece. On each upright was nailed a poster with the words: *Tierra o Muerte* — Land or Death, printed above a black and white image of the face of Emiliano Zapata, the Mexican revolutionary, his black handle-bar mustache drooping.

State wildlife officers in green uniforms and half-a-dozen state police officers in black flak jackets, the butts of shotguns resting on their hips, formed a human barricade. A state police officer held up a hand.

"You need a press pass to go any further," he said.

Jackson pulled out his wallet and produced a laminated card with PRESS in large capital letters and his black-and-white mugshot.

The officer looked at it from behind his dark sunglasses. "It's expired."

Jackson shrugged and squinted. "Sorry. Slipped my mind." He looked past the fence gate and up the rutted road to the encampment visible through the pine and aspen trees.

The cop drew a deep breath and exhaled slowly, then waved him through.

Fifty yards beyond the gate, Jackson stopped at a second group of armed men, none of whom were police, who leaned menacingly against the trucks. A young man who Jackson guessed was only sixteen or seventeen years-old, pointed a shotgun at his chest. Jackson raised his hands slightly and said, "I'm with the press."

The young gunman lowered the barrel of his gun and eyed Jackson's camera bag. "*Abierta.*" Jackson opened it. After inspecting it, the kid stepped back. Jackson went on.

The encampment consisted of a large green tent, a pickup mounted with a live-in camper, and another small, pale green trailer parked in the trees. A television camera crew sat in the shade not far from a smoldering, rock-lined campfire.

Looking anxious, Antonia emerged from the trailer followed by a man in a black ski mask. They spoke quietly together while surveying the camp.

"We're going to get started here in a few minutes," she said.

The Channel Nine crew was coming up the road, followed by Donna Brock and Terry Collins.

"Here. Read this," Antonia said, handing Jackson a sheet of paper. He scanned the press release, which was headlined: "*Proclamacion del Cooperativo del Valle*".

"My God," Brock said breathlessly. "What's going on?" She had intense dark eyes and short, salt-and-pepper hair.

Jackson shrugged. "They're going to take us hostage."

Collins looked at him warily and shook his head in disgust. "That's not funny."

"Give us something to write about, wouldn't it?" Jackson smiled.

"I got plenty to write about," Collins said, scratching his beard.

A small dust devil swirled, picking up ashes from the fire, then grit, twigs and leaves and it danced toward the police. The officers bowed their heads and turned.

"Over here," Antonia said, motioning for Jackson and the others to come closer. The masked man stood beside her, wearing a striped T-shirt under a green hunting vest with shotgun shells in the loops along with a holstered military-style .45 caliber pistol. He stood with balled fists on his hips, scanning the scene like a commanding general.

"Thank you for coming," Antonia said more loudly than she needed. She had a thin, tough-looking face, but large, dark eyes. "I am Antonia Aguilar, director of *El Cooperativo*, which initiated this action. We are gathered here for one reason and one reason only. That reason is justice." From behind Antonia, a young boy paused in the doorway of the Airstream, then scampered down the wire mesh steps and ran to her, grabbing her leg. She stopped and glared at the boy, then patted his head gently.

Jackson clicked on his tape recorder and flipped his notebook open. On either side of him, television cameras were steadied and focused.

"You're standing on a land grant given to our ancestors by the

Mexican government more than a century ago." Her voice was sharp and loud. "This grant was recognized by the U.S. government under the Treaty of Guadalupe Hidalgo in 1848. But the land was stolen from us. Some of it ended up in private hands when it was taken from its rightful owners and their heirs. Some of it is now held by the state government." She cleared her throat. "We are peaceful people. We have tried to live with these injustices. Fencing off traditional grazing land for our flocks is one thing, but we will not tolerate the murder of our people. We have been forced to take this drastic action in order to reclaim what is rightfully ours."

She fell silent, leaving only the sound of the wind in the trees.

Jackson glanced over his shoulder to where the police watched.

"Now our leader, El Cuchillo, will speak to you," Antonia said.

The masked man stepped forward.

Jackson recognized the man's stocky build and suspected he was the same man who'd been at the shearing.

"I am El Cuchillo. On this very spot where we stand an important member of our community was murdered a week ago. We buried him last Sunday. He was a shepherd his whole life. The sheep he watched belong to the people of our village and of *El Cooperativo.* We have been using these pastures for generations."

He paused to look around.

"The Wildlife Department," he continued, "just put up this barbed wire fence around what they are calling the Johnson Wildlife Area."

He spat and pointed.

"They told us the land was now off-limits to our sheep so that the elk will have enough grass to eat, especially during calving season."

His voice grew louder.

"But in the summer, these same elk graze in our alfalfa and wheat fields. They eat the hay out of our barns in the winter."

He lifted his clenched fist over his head and pounded the air.

"We cannot even afford to buy the permits to hunt these elk. The only ones who can hunt the elk are *los ricos* from out-of-state." El Cuchillo fell silent.

Collins raised his hand.

"Is El Cuchillo your real name?"

El Cuchillo glared at him. "Yes."

"Why the mask?"

"My identity will remain secret to protect my friends and family."

"An old shepherd was murdered?" Brock asked.

"His body was found here beside this fence." El Cuchillo pointed a thick finger to where the fence had been cut. "He was shot in the back. This young boy, Manuelito, found him."

"Why would someone kill an old shepherd?" Brock asked.

El Cuchillo shrugged. "That is what we would like to know. Someone needs to pay for this crime."

"Do you think wildlife officers shot him?" Collins asked.

"We don't know for sure."

"Why did you call this press conference?" Brock asked.

El Cuchillo scratched his cheek through his mask. "We want the state police to investigate the murder. We want the murderer or murderers brought to justice. We are also demanding that the Wildlife Department remove this fence and let us graze our sheep here as we have done for more than a century."

"And if they don't?" Brock asked.

"We are armed and prepared to stay here until our demands are met."

※6※

Santa Fe

Black metallic ivy leaves curled out from steel vines that snaked around the bars of the gate. It was skillfully wrought iron work. Jackson ran a finger along the edge of a leaf, examining the scored veins. This forged ivy stood the best chance of survival here in the high desert, he thought.

Jackson froze momentarily, then jumped backwards, stumbling as a pair of growling mastiffs, shoulder to shoulder, heads lowered, charged down the asphalt drive. Jackson scrambled back toward his truck as the beasts leapt violently against the high gate, drool flying from their muzzles. They repeatedly slammed against the metal, growing and biting it, bloodying their gums.

After a few minutes, the dogs slowed, pacing back and forth, occasionally barking and pausing to lick themselves. Any movement by Jackson sent the dogs into more frenzied snarling and barking. They had no way to break through the gate, thank God, Jackson thought. A tall, chain-link fence topped with three strands of barbed wire stretched in both directions from the gate, disappearing up the surrounding hills and between the piñon trees.

Cautiously he went to the call box in the wall. The breath of the barking dogs was foul and hot as he followed the instructions above the numbered buttons to leave a message. He felt foolish shouting over the deafening barks and into perforated plate covering the voice box.

"Uh, this is Luke Jackson. It's, uh, three-fifteen and, uh, I'm here to pick up Luna for the weekend. Margo? Are you here? This is when and where you told me to be. Fredrickson's new house."

Jackson retreated and leaned against the hood of his small pickup truck. He gazed at the neighboring two- and three-story stucco mansions that towered above the scrubby piñon pines. He used a hand to shield his eyes from hot sun. At better than a million dollars each, tens of millions of dollars in real estate were scattered throughout these foothills of the Sangre de Cristo Mountains.

After repeatedly pushing the buzzer on the call box and getting no response, he checked the messages on his cell phone. One from Margo. It had come at a few minutes after nine that morning, but Jackson hadn't noticed it. Margo said she wondered why he wasn't picking up his calls and then said that she and Jim had to leave earlier than expected and that unless he called within the next twenty minutes, they were taking Luna with them. Luna was sorry to have missed him, but was excited to be going to San Diego because they were going to see Shamu the whale at SeaWorld on Saturday. They would return Sunday evening, she said, and he could see Luna the following weekend if he liked, or whenever. Just call, she said. Jackson's stomach soured.

He steadied his gaze as the beasts growled at him from behind the gate. He threw a baseball-size rock as hard as he could. The rock hit the gate, bounced through the wrought iron, and dropped harmlessly to the asphalt. A second smaller one sailed through the gate and hit one of the dogs. It yelped and both retreated, tails between their legs, pausing after ten yards to face him. Jackson ran to the gate, shook it, and screamed. It launched the dogs into another frenzy.

§

His throat was sore as he took a couple deep swallows from his beer. Three women, two of them Hispanic, sat at the far end of the crescent-shaped bar, talking, glancing. One looked familiar. He recognized one and realized she was Ariel, the massage therapist. He smiled and nodded.

Ariel looked away.

Jackson looked again at the television screen on the wall where basketball players ran up and down the court, shooting, rebounding, slam-dunking.

He looked again at the women at the end of the bar. It was definitely Ariel. She looked lovely. He sipped.

On the television screen, another player slam-dunked the basketball and the crowd stood, fists pumping the air.

Ariel slipped off her seat and walked past him toward the restrooms. He pretended not to notice, but a few minutes later, when she reappeared and passed behind him, he called out. "Ariel?"

She paused and looked at him blankly.

"Remember me?" he asked.

She stared quizzically. "Not really."

"At the hot springs. Saturday. You gave me a massage."

She smiled. "Oh yeah." She squinted, trying to remember. "You're the journalist, right?"

"Yes. Luke Jackson." He extended a hand. "Thanks for the massage. I felt like a new man."

"That's the way it's supposed to be," she said.

"I could use another one."

"Come up to the springs again."

Jackson shrugged. "I will."

The conversation lapsed awkwardly.

"Out for a night on the town?"

Ariel flushed slightly. "Not really. Well sort of. We came for the *tapas*, actually."

"Me, too. Come for the tapas. Stay for the margaritas."

"It's my one indulgence," she said.

Jackson nodded agreeably. "Well, nice meeting you. Again."

"Likewise," she said.

Jackson watched her as Ariel rejoined her two friends, who glanced at him after they took seats at a table that had just cleared. Ariel put her glass down and looked at Jackson, motioning to an empty chair.

He smiled broadly, collected his drink, and took a seat in the remaining empty chair.

"This is Angel and this is Yvonne," Ariel said, motioning to her friends.

"Hi. I'm Luke Jackson."

They nodded.

"Is this ladies night out?" he asked.

"Got to do it," said Angel. She had thick, full, jet black hair and heavy makeup. Her lips were bright red.

"Our boyfriends are coming," Yvonne said, "if they're not all drunk already." She flashed her dark eyes.

"Let's hope not," Jackson said. His beer bottle empty, he motioned to the waitress who was nearby and ordered another round.

"Have something," Yvonne said to Ariel. "It won't kill you."

"Okay," Ariel said. "I'll have a white wine."

The waitress reached for Ariel's glass of lemon water, but Ariel put her hand over it.

"You have a long commute from Santa Fe," Jackson said.

"Actually I live near Ojo Caliente," Ariel said.

"Do you like it?"

"It's okay. The rent is cheap, but I've been robbed twice. They took my stereo and television. I don't really care, though." She sighed.

"Who?"

"I don't know."

"Did you call the police?"

"I called. They told me to put better locks on my doors and windows."

"What about your landlord?"

"My landlord lives next door. He said he never saw anything." She looked down at the table.

"I was back up in the north yesterday working on a story about the land grant protest."

"There's a land grant protest going on up there?" She shook her head slightly, unaware of it. Her tawny hair was spread down over her shoulders. She lifted the glass of wine to her lips and focused on him.

"That's right," Jackson said. "I forgot that you don't follow the news, it being repetitive and all."

She nodded. "I'm happier that way."

The waitress took their tapas orders.

"I'm also doing another story that may be more to your liking," he said. "It's on the wool growers and the weavers in the northern communities."

Ariel brightened. "They make wonderful things, don't they!"

Jackson nodded. "I took pictures of the sheep shearing up there this week."

"Oh, I wish I could have seen that."

"It's pretty simple really. They sheer it off the sheep, wash it, and dye it. Then they dry it, spin it, and weave it."

"It all sounds so wonderful. I love it up there. People are so...so close to the earth."

"I guess."

"You're really lucky, you know. You get to do a lot of interesting things."

"It can be a grind."

The tapas came just as Yvonne and Angel's boyfriends came. One was a hulking man, who wore tight, clean jeans, a western shirt and a cowboy hat. He had big, rough hands. His buddy was smaller and said he worked for the state fish and wildlife department. They'd been drinking, but were in good spirits and teased the women about eating.

One of the men suggested they all go to El Farol, a bar on Canyon Road, where they could dance. Ariel and her friends readily agreed, and they immediately signaled for the bill, which they paid, then rose to leave.

Jackson followed their small caravan and parked in the gravel lot across the street and close to the bar. Live music and loud bar noise spilled out into the street from the open bar door where a big man with a thick, blond beard collected a cover charge.

After entering the bar, Yvonne and her boyfriend worked their way onto the crowded dance floor as Jackson and the others found empty chairs at a large table covered with beer glasses and bottles. When the song ended, the band took a break.

"We should have danced when we had the chance," Jackson said to Ariel.

"There'll be another set," she said.

"Have you been to the Santuario de Chimayo?" he asked.

"Of course," she said. "It's one of the most sacred places in the world."

Jackson nodded. "I'm going up there tomorrow to interview the priest. They have a big heroin problem in that town."

"Is that what you're going to write about?"

"I don't know, yet. I need to go up there first and look around."

Later, after dancing, Jackson walked Ariel to her car. He bent to kiss her, but she gave him her cheek.

※7※

Santa Fe

"Faustino Fernandez," Jackson said to the receptionist. He stood at her desk in the office off the hallway of the three-story, territorial style state office building a couple of blocks from the capitol. She was an aging woman with tortoise shell colored combs stuck in graying hair. She looked away from her laptop computer screen and squinted, as if in pain. "Is he expecting you?"

"Yes."

"Then sign in," she said, pointing to a sheet on a clipboard at the corner of her desk. The woman picked up her office phone and called Fernandez. "There's someone here to see you," she said. "A mister Jackson."

She listened for a moment, then hung up and motioned down the hallway. "He'll meet you in the conference room. It's on your right," she said.

Portraits of men with flowing mustaches, starched collars, and heavy wool coats lined the hallway walls, each of whom had played prominent roles in the history of New Mexico and the American Southwest. Jackson stepped into the conference room, took out his notebook, and settled into one of high-backed leather chairs.

His mind drifted as he thought about his daughter Luna, who had called him the night before, bubbling about her trip to California, how she saw Shamu the killer whale and all the other sea creatures, and how she had such a wonderful time had stayed at Jim's house with a swimming pool, a tennis court, and had her own room with a big-screen television. Jim even had his own room for watching movies.

Jackson's musings were interrupted when a short, balding man with chubby cheeks, a heavy beard, and wide-set eyes hurried up to him and stammered out his name.

"Faustino Fernandez," he said, extending a thick hand. "Have we met before?"

"It's possible," Jackson said. "I work for *The New Mexican* newspaper."

"Yes, now I remember," Fernandez said. "Well, tell me what's happening up at Tierra Amarilla? All I know is what I read in the papers." He smiled.

Jackson nodded. "They've armed themselves and demand access to the land grant they say was taken from their predecessors. I'd like to know more about the history of the land."

"A journalist who wants to get the facts?" Fernandez said. "Amazing." He had large eyes, wispy hair and massaged his face as if trying to wake up.

Jackson cleared his throat. "I let the facts tell the story."

Fernandez frowned and nodded. "So what would you like to know?"

"Well, is their land grant claim valid? Or, is this just a lot of bluster?"

Fernandez unwound a string that secured the flap to a fat, blue file folder. He carefully took out several old documents encased in clear plastic and put them on the table. The old, hand-made paper inside the plastic was grayed and the ink had faded, but Jackson could see the Spanish written with black ink and quill pen. Fernandez selected one and pushed it to Jackson.

"This is the original land grant made in 1832." He pointed to a name at the bottom. "It was made out to Señor Don Efrian Esquibel."

"One man?"

"Back in those days, not everyone knew how to read and write. They relied on anyone who was educated to sign their papers and represent them in legal matters. For those grantees, Esquibel was that man."

Jackson nodded and took notes.

"That means Esquibel and his heirs technically could claim it?"

Fernandez shook his head, no. "It's still a community land grant." He pointed to other names at the bottom of the document. "These are the co-signers. But not all of the grantee names are here."

"How do you know who the heirs are if their names aren't on it?"

"It's complicated."

Jackson shrugged.

"A lot of cross-referencing is needed," Fernandez said.

"What does that mean?"

"If people can prove some sort of connection to the grantees, they can make a claim."

"Connections? Like what?"

"Like any legal documents, deeds to property, voter registration, tax documents, and things like that."

"So, the grant itself is legitimate?"

"Of course." Fernandez narrowed his eyes. "But you need to understand about grants. Each member of the community got a parcel, about five acres, big enough for a house, a barn, a large garden, and a pasture for a couple of cows and horses, that sort of thing." His eyelids quivered. "Follow me so far?"

Jackson scrawled notes, flipped a page, and looked up.

"Most of the land in the grant, however, was held in common. The forests were logged as needed. Cattle and sheep were grazed in the common fields."

"So their land claim is valid."

Fernandez brushed perspiration from his upper lip. "If the land they're on was part of the grant's common area and if they can prove they're descendants of heirs, then yes, they might have a legitimate claim."

"It's that simple?"

Fernandez wiped a hand across his mouth again and sighed. "Back in eighteen forty-eight, what was then northern Mexico became part of the United States under the Treaty of Guadalupe Hidalgo. It included most of what is now the American Southwest, from west Texas all the way to the west coast, including Nevada, Utah and all of California."

"I'm aware of that," Jackson said, scribbling notes.

"The treaty said all existing Spanish and Mexican land grants would be recognized," Fernandez continued. "But communal land grants were not a recognized part of the American system of land ownership."

Jackson scribbled notes.

"So, when the U.S. Congress adopted the treaty, they struck the portion that recognized the land grants. Then later, in 1860, the Congress declared that the entire land grant belonged to a man named Efrian Esquibel."

Jackson scrawled then looked up. "What? How did that happen?"

Fernandez shrugged and shook his head. "By this time, the Santa Fe Trail had opened up. The next thing we know is that the land was sold to a Santa Fe lawyer named Thomas B. Catron."

"How did that happen?"

"We think he bought it from Esquibel."

"What happened to Esquibel?"

"He disappeared."

"But with the money?"

Fernandez nodded.

"What about the other land grant members?"

Fernandez sank into his chair. "They never knew what happened. They were left with only their small five-acre parcels...if they had a title. Meanwhile, Catron sold the common lands, including the pastures and the forests, to the railroad company. The company wanted the wood for railroad ties."

"But the land is now owned by the U.S. Forest Service. How did that happen?"

"After a series of private land sales, it was donated to the state as a wildlife preserve."

"So what about today's land claim?"

"They're about a hundred and thirty-five years too late. The only legitimate fix is for the U.S. Congress to change its mind, reverse its decision of eighteen sixty, and then try to sort out the chain of titles and give the land back to the heirs." Fernandez clasped his hands and leaned on his elbows.

Jackson was silent for a moment, then slowly closed his notebook and slipped it into his pocket. He leaned back. "So what do you think?"

A look of resignation filled Fernandez's face. "What you just heard was Fernandez the historian talking. I was born in El Valle. My father was born in El Valle. My grandfather was born in El Valle. You get the idea."

Jackson reached for the encased land grant and perused the signatories. His fingers stopped at F. Fernandez. He looked up.

Fernandez beamed.

"You're an heir."

He nodded.

"You have papers?"

He nodded.

"Your people got screwed out of their land."

He frowned and nodded. "Yes, we did."

§

A stuffed black bear and a big horned sheep stood sentinel inside the state Department of Wildlife offices. Jackson walked down a long, dark hallway of terra cotta tiles to an office marked Public Affairs. After checking in with the secretary, Jackson was motioned into an inner office with a cluttered desk. The department's publicist, John Cranston, was fit, but with his thinning gray hair, looked older than Jackson remembered.

Standing with Cranston was a man who introduced himself as Morton McDowell. McDowell combed hair across a bald spot on top and wore a white shirt with a skinny dark tie. After introductions, they gazed at the topography map already spread across Cranston's desk.

"The Johnson Wildlife Area was donated to the state in nineteen twenty-two as a permanent game preserve by W.R. Johnson," McDowell said.

"Who liked to hunt elk," Cranston said.

McDowell nodded. "It was set aside specifically for hunting."

"No grazing?"

"I don't know what kind of verbal agreements Johnson might have made with local people, but grazing was never a part of the deal. There hasn't been any sheep on that land, officially anyway, for more than sixty years."

"Who built the fence?"

"The department did," Cranston said. "That group up there, *El Cooperativo*, has been running sheep up there for a number of years. We come around every once in a while and have to chase them off. We finally built a fence. We're just trying to protect the wildlife in the area."

"The people up there who say they're heirs of the land grant claim your men shot and killed the old man, the shepherd."

McDowell turned a deep red. "You not going to print that, are you?"

"Of course. It's what they said."

"What do you think?" McDowell asked.

"I'm asking you."

McDowell tugged at the knot of his tie. "What kind of question is that?" He scowled and shook his head in disgust. "We're wildlife officers, not gunslingers."

"Your men carry guns."

"We deal with a lot of heavily armed people. It's for our own protection."

"So who do you think shot the old man?"

McDowell clenched his teeth and exhaled through his nose. He looked at Cranston.

"Off the record?" Cranston asked.

"Sure." Jackson put his notebook on his lap and fiddled with his pen.

"We're being set up," McDowell said. "They're gonna use public opinion to force the state to give 'em the land. Then they can do what they want with it. Probably sell it."

※8※

Chimayo, New Mexico

Jackson found the graveled lane that lead to Ariel's mobile home. Unable to get her off his mind, he felt compelled to visit. He was in the neighborhood doing a story on the upcoming annual Holy Week pilgrimage to the Santuario de Chimayo, which was just five miles from her mobile home. He parked near the black, wire mesh steps to her front door.

Three low-slung, customized cars were clustered at the mobile home next door. It was embellished with additions made of weathered wood and bare concrete block. Men wearing dark, deeply pleated pants and thin white undershirts, their eyes hidden behind narrow sunglasses and slicked-backed hair, leaned against the cars with crossed arms covered with tattoos. Some wore bandannas. One wore a hair net. They turned to watch him.

Their cars gleamed in the sun and sat only about six inches off the ground, with wide white-wall tires mounted on gold-spoked rims that extended outside the wheel wells. Two of the men swigged from bottles in brown paper bags. Jackson checked his watch. It was ten forty-three. Ariel's yard was nothing but a patch of dirt sprouting weeds and delineated by a rusted and sagging barbed wire fence. There was no car parked at her trailer, so he assumed she must be at work. He backed out and drove away.

The paved road to Chimayo followed the river, snaking under stout and leafy cottonwoods. On the other side of the river, a man drove a tractor slowly as he plowed moist soil. The pungent scent of fresh earth mingled with swirling white smoke as two men and a woman tended a small fire that burned the dried weeds of winter that choked an *acequia*, the irrigation ditch. As the woman raked the brown weeds into the smoldering ash, they flared, pushed by the wind, forcing her to step back. Then the flames quickly died.

Jackson continued along a dirt road, passing partly plastered adobe structures made of concrete and dusty river rock. He parked near the infamous *santuario* with its corrugated tin-covered steeples pointing into the clear blue sky. The modest structure, fronted by an aging, weathered and crooked cross tilted to the right, attracted pilgrims from around the world each Holy Week. A dust devil swirled toward him down the road, then danced around his car, coating it with dust as he hurriedly rolled up his windows.

A sign at the *santuario* parking lot read, "Lock your car. Not responsible for theft." He parked beside two vans painted with green lettering that proclaimed, First Berean Baptist Church of Beaumont, Texas. White-haired women and men, stoop-shouldered under windbreakers and sweaters, shuffled toward the church.

Jackson checked his pocket for a notebook and pen, then locked his truck.

The open flagstone courtyard of the chapel was surrounded by a plastered wall that matched the color of the chapel. He paused to touch the deeply weathered wooden doors that opened into the courtyard. Once they swung free, but now the doors were opened wide and set in concrete.

Jackson quietly stepped into the cavernous interior of the chapel.

The high blue walls of the interior were interspersed with floor-to-ceiling panels of individual retablos, each depicting a saint or martyr worthy of the parishioners' thoughts and prayers. The altar of the chapel was predominately blue, pink, and yellow with vertical designs surrounding a nearly life-size crucifix. The ceiling was marked by stout, brown *vigas*, the thick logs of ponderosa pine now stained and resting on the carved and rounded lintels jutting inward from the adobe walls.

Jackson walked reverently as he approached the altar, then past the last pew, turned right where he found a varnished door with a small placard: Office. He knocked and the door swung, as if opened by an unseen hand.

Inside, a diminutive figure dressed in clerical black and with a rigid, round white collar, sat at a desk, a telephone to his ear. He had thick graying hair and smiled, motioning for Jackson to sit down. The loose skin of his wrinkled neck wriggled as he spoke, and he quickly ended the conversation with an abrupt "thank you." He looked at Jackson with eyes enlarged by his thick-lensed glasses. "Welcome. What can I do for you?"

"I'm Luke Jackson. I'm a journalist from Santa Fe. I'm writing a story about the annual pilgrimage."

The priest looked at him for a long moment. "Who you work for?"

"*The New Mexican*. The Santa Fe newspaper."

The priest nodded. "Fine, fine. I know it. I'm Father Roque Larragoite, priest of this parish. It's spelled L-a-r-r-a-g-o-i-t-e. Just call me Father Roque. You like a tour?"

Jackson jotted down the spelling of the priest's name from his desk nameplate, then followed Father Roque across the rear of the chapel to where he paused at a large varnished cross propped in the corner. He rapped it with his knuckles. "This was carried all the way from Albuquerque. Such faith," he said, then stroked it gently.

The church floor was made of varnished flag stone and the walls were hand painted with scenes from the life of Christ. An old wood stove stood beside the altar, presided over by a life-sized Virgin of Guadalupe manikin. Father Roque looked at Jackson, expecting a question, but Jackson had none. A few of the devout, perhaps early arrivals for the pilgrimage, knelt in one of the rear pews with heads bowed, hands clasped in prayer.

Father Roque led Jackson into a candle-lit side room with a waxy, golden air. The walls were cluttered with hanging crutches, braces, and artificial arms and legs. A wheel chair was covered with blazing votive candles. Father Roque sighed. "I have seen miracles. People drop their burdens here. They walk away healed."

"Really? You've seen the lame walk?"

"People can be lame in many ways."

Jackson smiled. He wrote that down.

Father Roque walked into an even smaller adjoining room with a dirt floor where several people knelt around a hole, hands pawing dirt, some filing small glass vials. He leaned close to Jackson and whispered, "It's the holy dirt."

Jackson nodded.

"Many believe it has healing qualities," Father Roque said.

"Do you?" Jackson asked.

"With faith, all things are possible," Father Roque said.

A family of six crowded into the little room. Not noticing the dirt hole, a pudgy well-scrubbed boy about eleven- or twelve-years-old, stepped into it and thudded to the ground. Father Roque reached out instinctively and lifted the boy who struggled to right himself.

"André!" his mother blurted, pulling the boy from the priest's grasp.

The boy looked at the priest sheepishly, then at his mother.

"Watch where you're going," she said, quickly brushing his pants. "Look at you."

The family looked at each other, embarrassed.

"Let's go," the mother said, herding the children out.

Father Roque looked at Jackson and shrugged.

A moment later, an elderly woman stepped into the room and knelt beside the hole, scooping the sandy soil into a vial the size of a fat pen. She topped it with a small cork and dropped it into her purse. She crossed herself, glanced up at the priest, then stood and left.

Jackson squatted to touch the soil, rubbing it between his fingers. "Don't you run out?"

Father Roque motioned for him to follow as they walked out the back of the church and down a slope of sparse grass to an orchard. Father Roque paused to pull a cluster of blossoms to his nose and inhaled.

"God willing, we may have fruit this year," he said.

They walked to a gate secured by a chain and padlock in a chain-link fence topped with three strands of barbed wire that surrounded the orchard.

Father Roque pointed through the fence to an arroyo. "We refill the hole inside with sand from that arroyo out there. We bless it, of course, to make it sacred."

"Why this fence?"

Father Roque shook his head in disgust. "Bad people. There's too much theft. They take purses from women in the parking lot and run behind the church and down to this arroyo and into the hills." He gestured to the sparse piñon trees. "So we fenced it off." He sighed. "They even rob the offering box. We were being robbed every day." Father Roque pursed his lips, grabbed the fence and rattled it. "It cost us thousands. But the people who visit here, they were not safe."

"Do you fear for your safety?"

Father Roque smiled and shook his head. "My life is in God's hands. He will take me whenever he wants."

§

Ristras of dried and deeply red chili peppers hung under the eaves of the nearby store. The entry was shaded by a sloping roof of corrugated tin supported by two wooden posts. To the left of the double front doors were painted the words, SANTOS, WOODCARVING, and POPSICLES. To the right of the doors were small crucifixes and mural of the Virgin Mary who overlooked a collection of *bultos*, the carved wooden statuettes of various saints and Jesus.

Bright weavings and lacquered black crosses inlaid with golden straw covered the blue plastered walls inside the gift shop adjacent to the *santuario*. A young man with long, black hair slouched on a stool behind a cash register sitting atop a scratched glass countertop.

Jackson picked up a picture post card, a depiction of Christ on the cross with sorrowful eyes and a crown of jagged thorns. As he moved the card in the light, blood dripped down Christ's forehead. Jackson replaced the card.

Below the scratched and nearly opaque glass was a carved skeleton driving a cart pulled by oxen. He had seen reproductions of this many times before and it was always made him pause. He squatted to get a better look. "Death drives a cart," he said.

"Death drives whatever the hell it wants," the clerk said.

Jackson rose slowly. "Where can I find Estefan?"

"I'm Estefan."

"I'm a journalist from Santa Fe," Jackson said. "I'm writing an article about the pilgrimage. Can I talk to you for a minute?"

Estefan looked around and shrugged. "Sure."

Jackson pulled his notebook from his pocket. "Are you looking forward to this coming Easter weekend?"

"Of course."

"So what are your biggest selling items?"

"Depends. We sell a lot of food."

Estefan casually pointed his thumb to a beaded curtain across a doorway to more rooms behind the shop. "In there we sell religious things." He mashed the butt of his cigarette in a small metal ashtray and raked his fingers through shoulder-length black hair, pulling it back from his face.

"Father Roque told me there's a lot of theft during the pilgrimage."

"That's all you guys write about. Why don't you write something good for a change?" He looked at Jackson skeptically.

"Father Roque says it's the drug dealers."

Estefan shrugged. "Yeah."

"You know who they are?"

Estefan nodded. "Everyone knows." Estefan narrowed his eyes and looked past Jackson's shoulder to the front of the store. Jackson turned as the shop door opened and two middle-aged women entered. The women brushed past him, pushed aside the beaded curtain, and entered the back room.

Jackson followed them. They were inspecting a variety of what looked like crudely painted pictures of Christ on the cross hung on walls covered with simulated wood paneling. There were crosses and crucifixes of all sizes, some metallic and shiny, each with a small price tag. Candles lighted bookshelves. Pillows embroidered with Christ kneeling in prayer, his eyes uplifted to a light emanating from behind the clouds, were stacked against the wall.

In the corner of the room, a small boy was transfixed in front of television and watching cartoons. The boy took no note of the strangers who were in his living room.

Jackson introduced himself to the women as a reporter for the Santa Fe newspaper and asked if they'd answer a few questions for his article about the annual pilgrimage.

They nodded and smiled. "Of course. We come to the Chimayo chapel every year," said one, who identified herself as Rosa. "We couldn't come for Easter this year, so we're visiting early."

They looked at each other and smiled.

"Carmela rubs the holy dirt on her arthritis," Rosa said, motioning to her friend. "It keeps the pain away. We very much believe it works."

"What about the thieves?"

"We don't worry about that. Those people are everywhere. You have to go on with your life."

§

Back in Santa Fe later that day and again at his desk in the news room, Jackson called the Catholic parish. After being connected to a nun, he asked to talk to the priest in charge. The nun explained he was unavailable, but that she could probably answer his questions.

Jackson asked if the parish had many parishioners planning to walk to Chimayo on Saturday to arrive in time for the sunrise service Easter morning.

"Yes, we do," she said. "Usually several hundred each year."

"Don't you think it's dangerous?"

"Not really," she said.

"There's a lot of road traffic," Jackson said. "Then, there's the crime. I'm told there's a lot of theft."

"There's safety in numbers," she said.

After more conversation, Jackson smiled as he hung up. He had his lead. Safety in numbers, she'd said. He opened his lap-top computer, turned it on, and typed quickly.

> CHIMAYO, N.M. – For the faithful, there is safety in numbers.
>
> Dangerous traffic and fear of petty thefts will not stop the thousands of pilgrims who make the annual Easter trek from around the area to the Santuario de Chimayo seeking spiritual and physical renewal.
>
> Known for its magical healing powers, the centuries-old chapel has attracted not only the devout, but also thieves, prompting the parish to erect a chain-link fence topped with barbed wire around the church grounds.

Jackson sat back and reread what he'd written. It would do, he thought. It would do nicely. He leaned forward and continued to write.

nun, he asked to talk to the priest in charge. The nun explained he was unavailable, but that she could probably answer his questions.

Jackson asked if the parish had many parishioners planning to walk to Chimayo on Saturday to arrive in time for the sunrise service Easter morning.

"Yes, we do," she said. "Usually several hundred each year."

"Don't you think it's dangerous?"

"Not really," she said.

"There's a lot of road traffic," Jackson said. "Then, there's the crime. I'm told there's a lot of theft."

"There's safety in numbers," she said.

After more conversation, Jackson smiled as he hung up. He had his lead. Safety in numbers, she'd said. He opened his lap-top computer, turned it on, and typed quickly.

> CHIMAYO, N.M. – For the faithful, there is safety in numbers. Dangerous traffic and fear of petty thefts will not stop the thousands of pilgrims who make the annual Easter trek from around the area to the Santuario de Chimayo seeking spiritual and physical renewal.
>
> Known for its magical healing powers, the centuries-old chapel has attracted not only the devout but also thieves, prompting the parish to erect a chain-link fence topped with barbed wire around the church grounds.

Jackson sat back and reread what he'd written. It would do, he thought. It would do nicely. He leaned forward and continued to write.

※9※

Chimayo

The screen on the aluminum frame door was ripped and curled, the victim of a pry-bar. Jackson looked at it from inside Ariel's mobile home, then out to the empty fields and an old fence around an uncultivated field of grass. Alfalfa was growing in a field to the right.

Under the cover of darkness, anyone could approach the mobile home unnoticed, he thought. Most crime like theft was local, and of course, petty. You never really knew how bad it was because it was rarely reported. The sensational stuff like drive-by shootings and art heists grabbed the headlines. Stealing was a means to an end for some, not a question of right and wrong. Occasionally it was organized, but more often it was not. The thieves sold the stuff cheap from the trunk of their cars. Jackson took a deep breath.

The living room couch was worn and yellow and Ariel had covered it with a woven blanket. The couch arms were draped with dish towels. Her place was clean and simple, sparsely furnished. A silken, fringed scarf depicting the Virgin of Guadalupe was draped on the opposite wall, and below it was a stand with votive candles that hadn't been lighted. Bundles of dried herbs and flowers hung over the kitchen counter. The corner woodstove was cold.

Jackson opened a copy of the newspaper to show her his *santuario* story. They'd given it nice play and used a big file photo of a man lugging a large wooden cross along the roadside. Jackson sipped from a mug of herbal, honey-sweetened tea.

On the table beside his coffee mug was a hand-held police scanner that he'd borrowed from a photographer. Its small red light glowed, telling him the battery was low. He put it in the charger. The sizzle of frying came from the kitchen; spicy aroma floated in the air. Jackson inhaled and sighed. "Smells like burgers."

"Sort of," Ariel said, holding a frying pan in one hand and working a spatula with the other. She wore jeans and a faded orange T-shirt. He watched her at the stove as she turned, her light blue eyes steady, she noticed him noticing her. She flushed lightly. "Here, toss the salad." She handed him a bowl of fresh green lettuce. He sprinkled olive oil and vinegar over it and set the bowl beside two plates with hamburger buns open like hungry mouths.

"Veggie burgers?"

She nodded and flipping them.

"I had some of these at the hot springs."

She brushed away the rising griddle smoke.

Jackson sat at the Formica kitchen table with tiny gold and silver flecks sparkling in the worn surface. The table was beside a small bay window and looked across the fields and to the distant cottonwoods.

"Ready?" she asked, placing the patties on the buns putting the plate in front of him.

He used a plastic fork and spoon to serve the salad, then sprinkled salt and pepper on his patty and spread mustard on the bun. He took a bite. It wasn't meat, but tasted fine.

"This is good," he said with a mouthful. "It's nice of you to cook."

She dismissed the compliment with a glance. She bit into her bun and chewed carefully. "I appreciate you letting me come along. A night with the pilgrims. I mean I would never have done this unless, of course, I was walking with you."

He nodded. "I'm glad for the company. It can be dangerous for the walkers, though."

"That's something we all have to live with, don't we?"

"Some more than others."

She wrinkled her forehead and chewed politely. The sun burst through the clouds sending an orange light across the valley and in through the window. Ariel's tawny hair glowed. For a moment she seemed ethereal.

"Your hair looks auburn," he said. "You must have some Irish in you."

"100 percent," she said with a slight smile. "If ye don't mind me sayin' so," she added with a forced brogue.

He smiled. "Of course. With the name line McLaine, we should be eating corned beef and cabbage."

She shook her head. "A long time ago, I decided I was going to put only good things in my body. Meat is not one of them. We really don't need meat to be healthy. It's cruelty to animals."

"The beef industry would argue with that."

"People do so much harm to their bodies, it's amazing we survive at all. We keep putting toxins in our food, our water, and the air. It's amazing we're still alive. Our bodies are incredibly resilient."

Jackson nodded in agreement. He had smoked cigarettes when he was young, but had given that up, thank God.

"You know, when people clean themselves up, their life changes: attitude, awareness."

The glow from the sun had mellowed from yellow to pink. Her face was young, with faint creases at the edge of her eyes, pronounced by the angular light of the setting sun. Her lips had a slight downturn at the corners that made her look serious, almost sad.

"I've actually thought about writing a book about it," she said.

"The market is excellent for books like that. People are dying to make themselves better."

She grinned. "You said that right."

They finished dinner and he helped clear the table and ran dishwater in the sink. "We can let the dishes wait if you need to get going," she said.

"There's time." He soaped a sponge and washed the dishes quickly, placing them in the counter dish rack as she cleaned the kitchen table. He dried his hands on a dish towel then reached for her shoulder. She looked at him expectantly. "Thank you for dinner." He drew her close and she did not resist. He kissed her on the lips, but she did not open her mouth for him.

Moments later Jackson sat in his truck, letting it warm. The night had turned cold. He switched on the scanner below his dashboard and watched the green lights flash, one for each of nine channels. A voice crackled and a channel light stayed on. He adjusted the volume. The deadpan drawl reported that all was quiet, albeit increasingly busy. Jackson gathered from the chatter that road blocks had been set up a few miles from the chapel on the two main roads leading into the village. The move was meant to keep the drunk drivers off the roads and away from the pilgrims. He checked his watch. Nine-thirty. This was prime time, he thought. He went back into the house. "Ariel. Grab an extra sweater, just in case." She came out, shutting the door, leaving a light in the kitchen.

"You going to lock it?"

Ariel shrugged. "What's the point?" She looked into the darkness. "They'll just smash the door and break it open." She gazed at the sky and took a deep breath of the night air. "I can feel it already. This is a very holy night."

They climbed into his truck and found the winding highway crowded with cars, trucks, and vans, many with their warning lights flashing, moving slowly. Pilgrims walked on both sides, some alone, but most in groups, carrying flashlights, their jackets striped with reflective tape. The walkers looked ghostly, their faces drawn and tired.

Jackson slowed as he approached the end of a line of cars that extended as far as he could see ahead, red tail lights glowing. Yet more flashing red and blue lights marked a police roadblock. As he inched along, he turned up the volume on the police scanner and listened to the chatter.

"This is amazing," Ariel said. "Look at all these people."

Bright headlights suddenly came up behind him, stopping within inches of his pickup truck. The bright headlights glared in his rear-view mirror, momentarily blinding him. Jackson glanced at his side view mirror and saw the dim outline of over-sized truck tires and the thick, coiled springs of heavy duty lifters. The cab of the truck was four or five feet off the ground. He nosed closer to the car ahead of him.

The truck behind lurched forward, the engine revving, tires squealing. Jackson squinted again from the glare in his rearview mirror.

"This guy behind us is crazy," he mumbled to Ariel, then reached up and tilted the mirror downward. The engine of truck behind him raced again, the mufflers popping. Flares burned along the roadway up ahead, lighting the faces of law enforcement.

Jackson pulled forward then stopped beside a sheriff's deputy and rolled down his window.

The deputy put his face in the window. "Driver's license, registration, proof of insurance." The deputy sounded bored.

The truck behind Jackson rumbled anxiously.

Jackson pointed to the glove compartment. "There's an envelope in there marked registration," he said.

Ariel opened the compartment door, fished through the contents, then pulled out an envelope that she handed to Jackson. He extracted two pieces of paper that he handed to the officer, along with his press pass. "I'm covering this for *The New Mexican.* I need to speak to the commander, Lt. Steve Smith."

The deputy looked off into the darkness and pointed. "Pull over there."

Jackson edged to the side of the road, slipping between clusters of pilgrims, then stopped and looked over his shoulder.

The truck behind him had rolled forward and stopped, obscuring the deputy. The deputy shined his flashlight into the cab, silhouetting the driver and a woman, then waved them forward and stepped back. The truck engine revved loudly again. The truck jerked forward, fishtailed to the side of the road, scattering a knot of *santuario* walkers, then dropped off the shoulder and down a slope, headlights bouncing wildly, and disappeared behind some trees. Police scrambled to their cars, turning on lights and sirens.

"Here we go," Jackson said, jumping out of his truck and dodging through the crowd. Jackson heard crying. At the side of the road, a woman wailed as she knelt beside a body. Down the slope, a policeman's flashlight illuminated another body. Ten yards past the second body, Jackson could see the dim outline and glowing tail lights of the pickup truck, almost vertical, the nose down in the arroyo.

Smoke, dust and the smell of burned rubber hung in the air. Twirling red lights and the wail of sirens penetrated the darkness. Angular, needled-studded cholla cactus and chamisa bushes glowed red. Jackson stepped down the steep slope and paused near the body. It lay face down and didn't move, the clothes dusty, pants and jacket torn, wet with oozing blood. The body looked strangely misshaped.

Jackson stepped back, almost falling when he saw there was no head. His stomach knotted. "Oh, Jesus," he said. Ten feet away he saw the head, the skin partially ripped away from the face, exposing white bone. His legs felt weak. "Son of a bitch," he muttered, his stomach queasy. He took a few deep breaths to collect himself, then went toward the pickup to see if there were any survivors in the cab.

Two deputies were already tugging on the driver-side door. The nose of the truck was mashed and seemed buried in the sand.

The driver-side door suddenly sprang open, revealing the driver pinned back, the steering wheel mashed against his chest. His head was turned, eyes unfocused, with blood oozing from his mouth and nose. One of the deputies reached in and felt his wrist. "There's no pulse." He stepped back and spoke into the radio microphone that hung from the epaulet. "Got one dead down here. There's a woman in the cab, too. I can't tell with her yet."

A weak child's voice said, "mommy?" then was a silent. The child cried.

"My God," the deputy said. "There's a kid in there. Alive."

The other deputy scrambled to the passenger side door and jerked it, but it wouldn't open. "Hold on sweetheart. We're going to get you out of there."

"Mommy! Mommy! Mommy!" the child cried.

Gasping for breath, his heart pounding, Jackson climbed back up the slope. People had gathered near the body at the edge of the road where someone had thrown a blanket over the shoulders of the woman who now sobbed hysterically. She fought back as deputies tried to pull her away. Finally, her legs buckled and she fell to the ground.

The deputies yelled at people to keep moving, but they ignored the officers and paused to peer into the darkness as a strip of yellow plastic tape now was strung across the side of the road. Jackson ducked under it and returned to his truck. He climbed back into the driver's seat beside Ariel, who sat somberly, her arms folded, her head bowed.

She looked at him with tear-filled eyes that glinted red from the swirling lights. Jackson put his arm around her. She buried her face against him. His throat felt thick and his own eyes watered as he held her tight.

※10※

Chimayo

The sky was light when Jackson awoke. Ariel was in the corner of the truck cab, curled inside her jacket. She lifted her head for a moment, frowned at him, then closed her eyes. It had not been a good night for her and he regretted bringing her.

The deputies said two pilgrims were dead and had been carted off in a silent ambulance. The driver, with bloodied, mangled legs and a crushed chest, had been extracted from the smashed truck in the sandy arroyo. Jackson had seen and heard the empty beer cans clink as the man's body was pulled free.

The female passenger was alive, miraculously, but severely injured. In the flash and glare of the rescue lights, dirt, broken glass and dried blood matted her hair and her vacant eyes stared as she was strapped to a back board, her neck in a plastic collar. She was loaded onto a stretcher, carried up the slope, and shoved into the back of a waiting ambulance.

With her red lipstick, bloodied head, and deathly pale skin, she had looked like a mannequin.

The woman's child, a young girl, had been on the floor, stunned, bruised, and bloodied, yet miraculously alive.

Jackson shook his head to erase the vision, but the night's events would not leave him. He had slept fitfully for a few hours in the truck and now stepped into the chill of the morming air. He took a deep breath and tried to wake up, noticing the light frost on the car windshield. The sky was light.

"Ariel, look," he said softly.

She lifted her head slowly, staring at him with dull, glassy eyes, and groaned.

"Come on. Let's watch the sunrise service. That's why we came."

He stepped out, went around to her side of the truck, opened the door, and put an arm around her, kissing her softly on the cheek.

"It's all right," he said. "We'll get a cup of coffee. You'll feel better."

She stepped out unsteadily, stood for a moment, then stretched, blinking herself into consciousness. A fragile smile came to her face. He put his arm around her shoulders and she hugged his waist as they walked among the thickening crowd.

A small sea of humanity swarmed outside the church. Many had glassy eyes and euphoric smiles, some lost in their private reveries, oblivious to the events that clouded Jackson's mind. Potted palms and white lilies wrapped with purple tinfoil lined the church patio, reminding Jackson of a funeral service. Overhead, the rising sun painted the clouds in pink and orange, casting the church yard in a fiery glow.

Jackson had hoped to find coffee for Ariel in Estefan's store, but it was jammed with people. Jackson moved past it and to the left of the church to a makeshift structure with a hand painted sign announcing burritos.

He inched to the counter as the rich scent of chili and warming tortillas stirred his stomach. He ordered two coffees and two burritos, one with beef, the other with beans. Wrapped in tinfoil, their warmth was comforting in his hand, his coffees in the other.

He handed a cup of the steaming coffee and a wrapped burrito to Ariel. They ate standing at the roadside as hordes traipsed past. The thick, doughy tortilla filled with refried beans, chili, and shredded meat tasted like best food he'd ever eaten. He wanted another, but the crowd at the stand was now five deep. He and Ariel rejoined the crowd moving silently toward the chapel.

Outside the chapel, white-robed priests gathered at the doorway and moments later a droning, trance-like hymn arose from the crowd who'd managed to pack inside. Through the open doors and from his location, about fifty yards away, Jackson could make out a priest who swung a smoldering pot of incense at the end of a light chain, leaving puffs of incense in the air. At the altar, a boy dressed in a white robe lighted flickering candles.

Overhead, the sky brightened as streaks of orange sunlight touched the tree-covered hills behind the chapel and the shafts of light seemed to warm the chilled air. Jackson recognized the archbishop of Santa Fe,

Pedro Cisneros, who emerged from the doors of the chapel, his hands held ceremoniously out at his sides, palms up. He smiled and nodded. A murmur arose from the crowd, the sound coalescing into a hymn.

Ariel looked more alive now, her eyes bright once again. She held Jackson's arm tightly and rested her head against his shoulder.

The hymn, with its repetitive strain, built to a crescendo, then the crowd quieted.

Suddenly a woman in front of Jackson waved her arms wildly. "I see them!" she shouted. "I see them!" She pointed to the sky above the chapel and shouted, "The angels! The angels! I see them!"

A murmur rippled through the crowd.

"Yes. There they are," said a man, pointing excitedly as well. Others looked up in wonder at the clear morning air surrounding the chapel.

Jackson looked at Ariel. "See anything?"

She shook her head.

"There's three of them," the man proclaimed. "They shine. *Muy claro.*"

Jackson pulled out his notebook, moved close to the man, and tapped him on the shoulder. The man spun to look at him, his eyes glowing.

"I'm a reporter," Jackson said. "I'm with *The New Mexican* in Santa Fe. What's your name?"

The man looked at him with wild and distant eyes. He did not answer.

"Where you from?"

The man stared at him, not speaking.

"Have you seen angels before?"

The man shook his head, held up a hand to Jackson for him to back off, and turned away.

"The Lord God works in mysterious ways," Archbishop Cisneros said into his microphone, his voice echoing softly. "We are truly blessed in many ways."

Cisneros then asked the crowd to pray for God to welcome the souls of those who had died over the night. Ariel's eyes watered as she stared straight ahead, lost on the memory of the crash. Jackson put an arm around her shoulders and pulled her close. He had seen enough. They turned and walked back up the road.

§

Ariel revived as they approached the Ojo Caliente hot springs. It was crowded, but they managed to find a parking space, paid their entry fee, and were soon soaking in the mineral pools, not saying much, only hoping to soak away the events of the early morning.

After lunch, Jackson put his laptop on a table near the pool. He pondered a possible first sentence, debating whether to begin with the angels hovering the chapel or the dead pilgrims. He settled on both, noting ecstasy in the midst of tragedy. The words soon fell into place.

> CHIMAYO, N.M. – Three people died early Easter morning, victims of an apparent drunken driver, two of whom were struck and killed during the annual Easter pilgrimage to this ancient mountain village.
>
> The as-yet unidentified driver of the deadly truck was among the dead. He was pronounced dead on arrival at the Española hospital. One passenger in the truck is on life support and the second passenger, a child, was treated and kept for observation.
>
> The accident did not deter Archbishop Pedro Cisneros of Santa Fe from celebrating the traditional Easter sunrise mass at the chapel here, although he asked the pilgrims to pray for those who had died.
>
> As a crowd of about 2,000 celebrants attended the Easter mass, some claimed to see angels hovering above the Santuario de Chimayo.
>
> "We are blessed in many ways," Cisneros said after some pointed to the sky and described their angelic visions.

Jackson leaned back and stretched. It was a start. As he flipped through his notes, the dark events of the night came back, overpowering the afternoon light reflecting brightly.

※11※

Tierra Amarilla

Ariel sat with her arm out the window, surfing the wind with a flat hand. Sunglasses covered her eyes and the gusting wind tossed her hair.

Jackson turned off the main road to the village and stopped at the store in El Valle.

"What's this?" she asked.

"A weaving shop. I think you'll like it." It was a long way from where they'd just been, and Jackson wanted a dramatic change of scenery. "Why don't you browse? Find something you like, and I'll get it for you." He'd driven far out of their way, hoping the distraction would dispel the tragedy they'd witnessed. "There's someone here I need to talk to."

While Ariel happily browsed the chrome racks and wooden shelves of the wool store, Tienda Lana, Jackson asked for Antonia, who soon came through the doorway looking perturbed. Jackson was taken aback at her fierce demeanor, but when she recognized him, her face softened.

"Oh. It's you," she said. "I'm glad you're here."

Antonia took his arm and tugged him toward the kitchen. "We need to talk."

Jackson motioned to Ariel and said, "I'll just be a minute."

Antonia closed the office door and fear distorted her face. "The state is getting ready to move against us. We need to do something." She was shaking.

"What do you mean?"

"With guns. They're gonna say we started it. They'll wipe us out."

"I doubt that."

She gripped his forearm tightly and squeezed. She spoke slowly and deliberately through tight lips. "The police can do it and there's nothing we can do to stop them. We have vowed to fight to the end and we will."

Jackson was taken aback by her intensity. Her grip hurt.

"It just doesn't make any sense, Antonia," he said. "Public opinion will be against them. The governor wouldn't do something like that. Move a SWAT team against a group of peaceful sheep ranchers? It'd be a public relations nightmare. The only possible justification he could have is if you shoot a state patrolman or someone like that."

She shook her head as if he didn't understand. "They'll kill someone and blame us. They just need an excuse." She paused, her face filled with fear. "But we will never shoot first. You should talk to El Cuchillo. The governor is having a press conference tomorrow. You should be there, too. But first go talk to El Cuchillo."

§

The camp looked deserted, more lonely and secluded than Jackson remembered. He rubbed his arm where Antonia had gripped him. Her crazed look had been frightening and it haunted him as he slowed to rumble across the cattle guard. The government vehicles were gone, the state police were gone, and the camp had no guards. Jackson inexplicably felt apprehensive and for a moment thought maybe Antonia's fear was justified. Maybe police had wiped out the camp already. He parked next to a battered, orange pickup truck. As he got out, a young man came running at him with a rifle in his hands. Jackson froze.

"What are you doing here?" the young man barked in a heavy Spanish accent.

Jackson looked at him. "I came to see El Cuchillo."

"Who are you?"

"I'm a reporter, a friend of Antonia's. She told me to come here, to talk to him. I was up here a few days ago."

The young man nodded, looking less hostile. His hands gripping the rifle were dirty and he had curious eyes. A worn baseball cap sat off center on his head and a wooden match protruded from the corner of his mouth under a wispy mustache. "Wait here." He walked away quickly.

Jackson turned to Ariel and shook his head in disgust. Jackson fished through his briefcase for his tape recorder and notebook. By the time he found them, the young man had returned and was waving the rifle, motioning for Jackson to follow. Jackson took Ariel by the hand as they walked.

A heavy iron grate across a large fire pit supported a greasy skillet and large blue enamel coffee pot. Wearing his ski mask, El Cuchillo emerged from the trailer and stood at the fire pit, legs apart, fists planted on his hips. "State your business," he said sharply. Jackson was puzzled at the gruff manner.

"Antonia asked me to talk to you. Something about the governor." El Cuchillo looked impassively at him and then Ariel. "This is my friend, Ariel."

"What do you want to know about the governor?" El Cuchillo said stiffly.

Jackson sighed and looked off into the distance. He felt now that he was being used in what was becoming a tug-of-war for public opinion. If the governor was smart, Jackson thought, he'd ignore this whole thing and it would go away. But then it wouldn't go away if the press kept writing about it. El Cuchillo needed Jackson, but Jackson didn't need to put up with his brusque behavior.

"Look," Jackson said, lowering his notebook, "I don't need to be here."

El Cuchillo jerked back in surprise. His face slowly softened and he nodded.

"Antonia tells me the governor is having a press conference," Jackson said. "Do you have any idea what it is about?"

"The governor is going to issue an ultimatum," El Cuchillo said quietly. "He's going to tell us to move off the land. That we are trespassing on state property."

Jackson sighed and squinted. By having a press conference, the governor was taking this protest seriously. That meant he was also taking El Cuchillo seriously. Something probably was in the works. The governor's a fool, Jackson thought, if he moves against these people.

"Unfortunately, the governor is very confused," El Cuchillo said. "We will not be intimidated. The state is trespassing on communal grazing lands of the El Valle Grant." El Cuchillo swept his arm grandly. "These lands that were given to the people of El Valle by the Mexican government many years ago. The existence of grant papers proves our claims."

Jackson waved his notebook at El Cuchillo. "Hold on a minute. The historical facts are that a guy named Esquibel, whose name is on the grant, claimed he owned the land in the 1860s. That's when he sold it."

El Cuchillo stiffened, then slowly lifted a hand. "It means nothing! Esquibel was as poor man with a weak spirit. The dirty gringo lawyers told him that if he signed papers that the land was his, they would buy it from him. Esquibel would be a rich man. But Esquibel is not at fault. The fact is that the people had their land stolen. It must be returned. The time is now! *Es tiempo!*"

"The land has been sold and resold and much of it officially belongs to the government. You can't turn back the hands of time."

"We...we...it is not our problem if the United States government made a stupid mistake and said that Esquibel was the legal owner of the land. The Treaty of Guadalupe Hidalgo recognized legitimate land grants. We are the heirs. The property is rightfully ours. If the government does not recognize our claim, then we do not recognize the authority of the United States government. This land is still part of Mexico." El Cuchillo stomped a foot raising a puff of dust. He pointed to a tall wooden pole at the edge of the camp on which hung the white, green, and red flag of Mexico.

Jackson gazed at the limp flag. "I bet the Mexican government will be happy to hear this."

El Cuchillo scratched a cheek through the mask. "They already know about it. We have our contacts."

"I need to go now to hear what the governor is going to say," Jackson said. "Is there a way I could reach you later for a comment?"

"I told you everything you need for now."

"We'll see." Jackson looked at Ariel and nodded toward the truck. He looked again at El Cuchillo. "What if the governor tries to force you off this land?"

"I hope the governor would not be so stupid."

§

On the way back, Ariel said she thought El Cuchillo was interesting, but scary. Men with guns. She didn't like it at all. The protest was doomed, she said.

It was more complicated than that, Jackson said. There were historical issues at stake.

Ariel rolled her eyes.

When Jackson dropped Ariel off at her house, they found no signs that her trailer had been broken into again. But they'd left the front door unlocked. They looked around inside for a few minutes, but nothing seemed to be missing. He kissed her good-bye.

※12※

A couple of days later, Jackson sped north through Tesuque where the road snaked under towering cottonwoods, now in full leaf, and then on to Chimayo. Ariel's battered old Saab was in her dirt drive. He parked behind it and knocked on her rattling screen door. Silence. He knocked again. She slowly opened the door behind the screen door and looked at him with red, swollen eyes. "It's you," she said in a hoarse voice, dropping her eyes.

"What happened?" Jackson asked, horrified. She retreated weakly, collapsed onto her knees, and burst into sobs. Jackson crouched and slipped his arms under her, carrying her to couch. He brushed back her hair and saw a swollen eye, bruised cheek, puffy lips, scratched arms. "What the hell?" he mumbled. His stomach knotted. She had been beaten. He did not want to think of rape. "Ariel," he said softly.

She buried her face in his shoulder.

He held her carefully, stroking her hair. "It'll be all right. It'll be all right." Her body shook, refusing to be calmed. "How did this happen?"

"I was in bed, asleep," she said haltingly, her body shaking. "I woke up. A man was in my room."

"What did he look like?"

"It was dark...he was on my bed." She covered her face with her hands. "He said he was going to give me what I needed...I was so scared...." She clutched him, sobbing.

He held her close and whispered, "Relax, relax. It's all right, now."

"He was on top of me...the blankets were between me and him...I struggled...I pushed him off...." She started to laugh, slightly hysterical, then stopped. "I tried to run... he grabbed me...he hit me...I fought with him...I started to scream as loud as I could, but he kept chasing me, grabbing me...." She sobbed into her hands. "I hit him, hard...he was surprised. Then he came at me. I kicked him, but he wouldn't stop." After a while she gathered herself, sighing deeply.

Jackson felt sick. "Did he rape you?"

She looked at him through watery, swollen eyes and shook her head.

"Did you call the police?"

She nodded. "I sat in the living room all night with the lights on. I was afraid he would come back."

The screen door rattled loudly. They turned to it.

A short, very heavy-set uniformed sheriff deputy with a brown baseball cap stood on the bottom step and held a metallic clipboard. "Is this the residence of Ariel McLaine?"

"Yes," Jackson said.

"Someone reported an assault."

Jackson waved him in. The officer's black gun-belt creaked slightly as he walked, as if the wide, black belt kept his belly from spilling out. His brass name tag read Cpl. Lucero. Without asking, he settled onto the thinly padded green chair and gazed sympathetically. He ran a hand over his crew cut and pulled out a ball-point pen. "You need to tell me in detail what happened." He looked at Ariel, then at Jackson. "We can do it privately, if you prefer."

"It's okay. He's a friend. He knows."

She explained it all, stopping frequently to cry. Lucero pushed her for the man's description, but all she could say was that the man was dark, may have had a thin mustache, was slight, but strong. He reeked of booze, she said. Lucero laboriously wrote it all down, as if unaccustomed to holding a pen.

When she had finished, Lucero rose, crossed the room, and examined the broken bedroom window. The aluminum frame was bent, and looked like it had been pried with a crow bar. Her assailant had left by the front door, disappearing into the darkness, Ariel said. Lucero tapped the window. "This ought to be fixed," he said matter-of-factly.

That's not helpful advice, Jackson thought.

"It's always been like that," she said dully. "I spoke to the landlord, but he did nothing."

"Who's that?"

She nodded to the small ramshackle adobe house not far away. "Victorio Vigil."

Lucero nodded. "Rough family. Is old man Vigil still around?"

Ariel shrugged.

Outside, Lucero groaned as he bent to examine the shoe prints in the dirt below the window. "Nikes," he said. Squatting, resting the clipboard on his knee, he sketched the shoe print on a blank page. He strained to stand. "Well, that ought to do it."

"Aren't you going to take fingerprints?"

Lucero shook his head slowly. "Not much use, really, unless I can get a good clean print on a piece of glass or something. From what I see, there's not much chance of that." He looked at Jackson, then Ariel, and shrugged. "This shoe is good, though. I'll try to match it with some others we have on file."

"You can't arrest someone for wearing Nikes," Jackson said.

"No. But if we can match this with a description of someone in other incidents like this, we might dig up some suspects and get a positive ID. Then maybe we can make an arrest. It takes time." He looked at Ariel. "You been checked out at the hospital yet?"

Ariel's eyes filled with tears.

Lucero's face was pained. He brushed a trickle of sweat from the side of his face. "I think I have all I need."

Lucero took Jackson's mobile phone number. Jackson followed Lucero out to his cruiser. Lucero paused when he noticed three customized low riders parked next door. Deafening bass sounds pounded the air, drowning a voice spouting profane lyrics.

"Wait a minute," Lucero said. Hitching up his gun belt, he ambled toward the music.

Pounding, thumping bass sounds were deafening. The scent of marijuana smoke wafted. Three young men and two women, faces thick with makeup, leaned against their cars and ignored Lucero, who stopped in front of them. One reached into his car and turned down the music. One wore a hairnet pulled tight over his slick, black hair. He wore narrow sunglasses and had a thin mustache.

"I'm investigating a break-in and an assault. Last night, next door," Lucero said, motioning to Ariel's house with his clip board. "Any of you hear or see anything suspicious last night?"

One choked out a laugh. "No, bro. We weren't even here. We were partyin', weren't we?" he said to his friends. They all laughed and mumbled in agreement. Lucero was expressionless. The car interiors were plush, deeply padded and cluttered with empty beer cans and empty pint whiskey bottles. One wore canvas shoes, another wore patent leather loafers edged with mud. The other wore Nike high tops and bunched, baggy pants.

"The woman's had some break-ins before. You know anything about that?" Lucero asked.

No one spoke, eyes downcast, as if the ground was suddenly interesting. One crossed his arms and flexed his fingers. "This is a rough neighborhood, bro," he said with a toothy grin.

Lucero shook his head in disgust. "Well, we found some footprints outside the house that look like those Nike shoes," Lucero said, pointing to the speaker's feet.

The smile disappeared. He looked down at his feet, then slowly looked up at Lucero. "You accusin' me of somethin'?"

"Just looking for some information. You're sure you didn't see anything last night?"

"I already told you we was partyin', man." He signed his hands again and looked away. "This is gettin' borin', man."

Lucero turned back to Jackson and shrugged. "Thanks for your time," he said to the group. "Let's go," he said to Jackson.

Back at Lucero's squad car, Jackson asked him about the Nikes that the talker was wearing, but Lucero only shrugged. "I can't arrest someone for wearing Nikes."

※13※

"May I have your insurance card?" the Santa Fe hospital receptionist asked, peering over the half-lenses of reading glasses.

"I don't have one," Jackson said, "and neither does she."

The woman stared with gray raptor eyes. "Well then, you will be expected to pay before you leave."

"We will," Jackson said emphatically. "How long before a doctor is free?"

The woman shifted her gaze toward the empty emergency room. "Well, not too long. We had our usual weekend carnage. It's pretty well mopped up by now."

Jackson smiled at the woman's cynicism.

"Have your friend fill this out, please, and I'll find a doctor," she said, sounding almost human. She wore a white nurse's dress under a turquoise sweater with the sleeves pushed up her forearms. She walked with a permanent forward lean, a rigid back, elbows protruding.

Ariel filled out the sheet of paper while Jackson distractedly pawed through the waiting room's spread of mangled magazines. Jackson picked up an old one claiming to have found the year's most interesting people: all movie stars. Jackson tossed it back on the table.

A half an hour later, a younger nurse in green hospital garb called Jackson into a small examining room off the emergency room. The doctor, a man in his late thirties and dressed in emergency room clothes, gestured at Jackson to sit. "You're Miss McLaine's friend?"

Jackson nodded.

"You're going to be taking care of her?"

Jackson shrugged.

"She's been through a lot," the doctor said seriously. "I assume this has been reported to the police?"

"The sheriff."

“She’s got a lot of swelling and bruising, typical of an assault. We did a vaginal examine. There’s some swelling tenderness and that indicates a rape attempt. She’s a strong, healthy young woman. It probably saved her.” The doctor paused. “I think the biggest problem now will be psychological. People react differently. I’m going to prescribe some mild sedatives. And, she should see a counselor.” He scribbled on a piece of paper, tore it from the pad and handed it to Jackson.

Ariel emerged from the dressing room and put on a forced smile, but her chin trembled.

Jackson took her in his arms. He felt helpless as Ariel melted against him and quietly sobbed. He could do little more than wonder why she had to be the victim. He felt angry at his helplessness and swore to himself to not let it go unanswered.

§

Outside the hot springs casita, Ariel lifted a hand to shade her eyes. “I’m fine. Really. Go do what you have to do. I’ll be all right.” She sounded convincing enough.

He hugged her and went to kiss her, but the left side of her mouth was swollen. “Take those sedatives. Get some rest, okay?”

She nodded.

He drove north and turned at the large white sign suspended between two posts: Rio Chama Ranch. A monstrous rack of elk antlers was affixed to it. He angled up a winding, well-graded road into heavy trees. Occasional green pastures opened on either side. Tight, five-strand fences disappeared into the woods. Fat, well-fed horses grazed.

He came to stables and sheds with tractors and equipment. The road forked and ended at a massive log building flanked by several smaller log cabins. Jackson parked beside an olive green Hummer in the crowded gravel lot. Television station vehicles and other cars were already there.

He checked his watch: 11:30. He was late. In the center of the compound an over-sized American flag hung limply from a flagpole. The place was strangely quiet. To his right a couple of cowboys rode by. In the distance, a riding lawn mower droned.

A young woman in tight blue jeans and a crisp western shirt opened the door as he was about to knock. Her fingernails and lipstick were bright red, her cowboy boots well-polished. “Can I help you?”

“I’m with the press. Here for the meeting with the governor.”

She nodded. "Let me show you to the conference room." To his left was a spacious living room with a stone fireplace, leather couches, Navajo blankets on the wall and racks of elk antlers. "Who are you with?"

"*The New Mexican.*"

"Thanks for coming," she said with feigned enthusiasm. She was about forty, Jackson guessed, dark hair, blue eyes. She directed him to a varnished door which he opened. In the room was a conference table lined with straight-back chairs and at the far end was a raised platform with a table. Television cameras were set up and all the usual members of the capital press corps were there.

He paused at a black-and-white photo on the wall of Ernest Hemingway beside a dead bull elk, holding the antlers erect, a rifle in the crook of his arm. There were photos of politicians and movie stars, each with a trophy elk. Some faces were foreign; some were Mafioso. Collins and Brock stood against the wall. Sandusky was beside a straight-back chair.

"I'd like to come here for a vacation," Sandusky said.

"Not for you, my dear," Brock said. "This place is for high-rollers."

"Movie stars, presidents," Jackson said. "You'd fit right in."

Sandusky scowled.

"This place is weird," Collins said. "Did you see those Hummers out there?"

"Nice, huh?" Jackson said. "I think I'll trade my truck in for one. Anyone got a spare 60 grand?"

"Gee. I'm a little short," Sandusky said.

Denise Engelhard, the governor's press secretary, entered and distributed copies of the governor's prepared statement. It was brief and called the land grant protest "an intolerable and lawless situation." Attached was a copy of a crudely drawn map showing the outlines of the Johnson Wildlife Area. The location of the camp was inside it and circled in red.

Moments later, a blond man in jeans, a white T-shirt and safari jacket entered followed by Gov. Jack Carrow, who was tall with thinning hair and angular features, and Herman Gonzales, the heavyset director of the state Wildlife Department. They took seats at a small table on the platform. They squinted as the camera lights flicked on.

"Welcome," Carrow said. He lacked his usual smiling, confident air. Beside him Gonzales locked and unlocked his thick fingers, then brushed his forehead with the back of his hand. Carrow read from the statement, speaking forcefully. "A group of people affiliated with the El Co-op-er-a-ti-vo of El Valle has established an armed camp on state land. This is trespassing, plain and simple, and a clear violation of state law. The group claims it is not subject to the laws of this land, but I am here to tell you that the law extends to all corners of New Mexico and the law will be enforced."

Carrow cleared his throat, looked around for a moment, then continued. "This group is being led by a masked man who goes by the name of El Cuchillo. He and his followers claim the right to graze their sheep on state land that many decades ago was set aside as prime elk habitat and made available to any and all licensed hunters. Their claims of historic grazing rights are unfounded. If grazing has been occurring on state lands in recent history, it has been done so illegally." He looked into the cameras. "We are calling on this group to vacate their camp and leave the Johnson Wildlife Area." He put his statement down and leaned back.

"Next," Carrow said, turning to a man standing to his side, "I'd like to introduce my friend, Carl Hanson, owner of this wonderful place."

Hanson had the weathered, tanned face of an outdoorsman. He nodded casually.

"The reason we're here today," Carrow continued, "is that Carl is very concerned about the situation that has developed over in El Valle. He has made a very generous offer to make several hundred acres of prime land available to the wool-grower's cooperative. He is willing to lease the land to them at market rates. I intend to carry this offer to the legitimate wool growers of El Valle this afternoon." He looked to Hanson. "I guess that's all unless you want to say something, Carl." Hanson shook his head.

"Why are you making this offer?" Brock asked.

"Being a rancher and a sportsman, I realize that land is essential to any successful sheep operation," Hanson said. He smiled, revealing white, even teeth. "It just doesn't happen otherwise." He chuckled softly, then suddenly became serious. "I guess I just want to be a good neighbor."

"The protesters claim the wildlife area is traditional grazing land and they have a right to it," Brock said, narrowing her gaze.

Hanson scowled. "Well, that's just not true. That area's been dedicated to wildlife as long as anyone can remember. Grazing sheep on it is illegal. I think the governor said that already."

"What about the elk?" Collins said.

"What about them?"

Collins scratched his beard. "The ranchers say the elk eat out of the pastures just about year round. Yet the sheep can't graze in the wildlife area in the spring."

Hanson sighed, leaned back, shook his head slightly, then leaned forward. "The elk were there first. Always have been. I don't know why it's suddenly a problem for some people. Besides, the elk are considered a valuable public resource and generate a lot of tourism and tax dollars for the communities of the north."

"Some of the sheep ranchers have said the state needs to compensate them for the damage the elk do to their fields," Sandusky said. "That's why they want free grazing on public lands."

"Look," Carrow interjected. "The state can't be running around paying people every time some wild animals do damage to private property."

"Would you be willing to let the ranchers graze their sheep on your land for free?" Sandusky asked Hanson.

Hanson shook his head. "There's no free lunch in America."

"Governor, what are you going to do if they don't leave?" Brock asked.

"We have to take this situation one step at a time," Carrow said.

"Will the state police be called in?" Sandusky asked.

"We have a lot of resources at our disposal."

"What about the National Guard?" Brock asked. "They've been used up here before."

"We are well aware of the history of northern New Mexico," Carrow replied curtly. "The land grant claimants say the state is responsible for the death, or the murder, of an old shepherd," Jackson said. "That's what prompted the protest in the first place. Can you comment on that?"

Carrow paled. "We are aware of that accusation and it is totally ridiculous. A wild fabrication that has no basis in fact." His voice rose. "It is nothing but a weak attempt to make the state look bad, a feeble excuse to claim state land." Carrow caught himself and lowered his voice. "But, like all such accusations, it is being taken seriously and we are investigating. Herman Gonzales may want to comment on that."

Gonzales sighed and leaned toward the microphones. "All our officers are trained to handle weapons in the line of duty. They are law enforcement officers. To accuse our officers of killing someone, even someone who may have been trespassing, is a serious accusation. Our officers would only shoot in self-defense."

"But you're not saying a wildlife officer did not kill the old man," Collins said.

Gonzales swallowed, looked at Carrow and then Engelhard, who shook her head. "Our department has done a thorough investigation and we have found that none of our officers were in the area. But, the investigation is on-going and we are cooperating fully with the state police."

"Thank you for coming," Engelhard interrupted. "The governor will be happy to take questions later today after he meets with members of the cooperative."

Disgusted, Jackson looked up to the ceiling and noticed a surveillance camera hung in the corner above the platform.

※14※

The sun shone brightly between the clouds. "I hate this," Jackson muttered to himself. Chasing the governor from one staged event to the next. Carrow was using the press, orchestrating it, trying to spin the evolving situation to his advantage. But there was little choice. As a reporter, he had to follow the governor and report on his movements. Sure, Jackson thought, I'll follow you, we all will, but don't count on the outcome.

Jackson parked beside the television trucks near the front of La Tienda Lana and followed the glow of camera lights to the back weaving room where Carrow stood awkwardly beside a loom and watched a young, dark-haired woman flick the trundle across the tightly-strung yarn. In the glare, she grinned, embarrassed. Jackson felt badly for her.

"Can you show me how to do that?" Carrow asked. She shrugged and slipped off her stool. Carrow hiked a leg onto the seat. Jackson lifted his camera, focused, and got a light reading. She worked the loom and the cameras clicked. But when Carrow mimicked her motions, he clumsily bumped her hands. He scowled, then grinned. "Well, thank you very much," he said abruptly. "I learned something today," then quickly stood. "See. You *can* teach an old dog new tricks."

Jackson shook his head and looked at Sandusky who did likewise.

"The *consejo* is here if you'd like to meet now," Antonia said, standing behind him, anxiously glancing from the governor and the cameras. The governor nodded. As Antonia and Carrow moved toward her office, reporters followed, but Engelhard quickly blocked their way, holding up her hand like a traffic cop.

"Sorry guys, it's private." She pulled the door closed and leaned back against it.

"Who's in there?" Brock barked.

"Ms. Aguilar, whom you just met, and a few sheep ranchers."

"Is Carrow going to meet with El Cuchillo?"

Engelhard shook her head, irritated. The camera lights lightened her powdered face and stiffly coifed hair. "Of course not. He's said before he won't negotiate under the threat of violence."

Yeah, right, Jackson thought. Officials refuse to negotiate if they know they can win without it.

"We came all the way up here to cover this meeting," Brock said. "Now we can't get in?"

"The governor wants to relay Hanson's offer in private. He's very sensitive to the needs of these people and he is willing to help them build a more viable wool growing industry in the north."

"Give it a rest, Denise," Brock said bitterly, folding her notebook and looking at the others in disgust. After a few groans, the group fell back, the cameras lights flicked off. Jackson walked outside to the store porch where Collins puffed on a cigarette. Across the crumbling pavement was an abandoned adobe building, windows boarded shut, rusted nails staining the grayed wood. "What do people do here?" Collins asked, not really caring.

Jackson shrugged. "Raise sheep. Hunt. Fish. There's a fish hatchery around here someplace." He looked down the road to the church, its white spire jutting into the blue sky. It was quiet, lonely. The governor's visit was definitely the biggest event in the village in years, but nobody had showed. Only the press. And Carrow didn't notice, probably didn't care. He'd get his photo in the paper, a story about his peace-making efforts, and look like a reasonable guy.

"Nice and quiet here," Collins said, flicking his cigarette butt into the street.

Jackson nodded. A swirl of dust danced down the street. Cars sped past on the highway beyond the village. He thought of Ariel, of her bruised and battered face, standing there in the sunlight. Some people are animals, he thought, and need to be treated like animals. Punished, and punished severely. Jesus, he thought, I'm beginning to sound like a conservative.

Jackson checked his watch. Time dragged. This was the tough part, doing nothing, waiting for someone to say something or announced something, so he could scramble and write a story. After nearly an hour, he had made three rounds of the store and fondled most of the merchandise twice. The television reporters and cameramen lounged on the porch. In the back room, a half-dozen women worked the looms, the rhythmic clacking and squeaking filling the air. Jackson casually watched the woman to whom Carrow had talked. She was young, had a round face, large eyes and her dark hair was pulled back in ponytail. She noticed him watching, and lowered her eyes. "Hi, I'm Luke Jackson with *The New Mexican* newspaper in Santa Fe."

She looked up, surprised that he was talking to her.

"How'd you like the governor?"

She shrugged and smiled bashfully. "He's all right."

Not much of an endorsement, Jackson thought. She was humble, modest, and would say nothing rather than criticize. "Do you think he could ever learn to weave?"

She laughed lightly and leaned forward. "He has to learn to relax."

Jackson smiled. That's an understatement, he thought. She looked to her friends and said something in Spanish that made the other women laugh. Jackson looked at her quizzically, then jotted down her earlier comment. Carrow had not talked with her, Jackson realized, but had only used her for press coverage. "How long have you been doing this?"

"Most of my life," she said. "I've been here for two years now, ever since the store opened."

"Do you make any money at it?"

She shrugged. "Some. There's no jobs around here, so this is very important for us."

"What does your husband do?"

"He teaches over at the elementary school. He's off during the summer, which is when it gets busy for me, so it works out pretty good."

"What do you think about the grazing?"

She stopped. "It's not right that they stop us from grazing our sheep there. Without the sheep, there is no wool, without the wool...."

Her comments were interrupted by the opening of the office door. Carrow emerged, scowling, and strode past, head bowed.

"Excuse me," Jackson said, trailing him. Carrow went straight through the store and out to his car. On the porch, cameramen jumped and scrambled for their cameras. Others called out to Carrow, who stopped at his Lincoln. "All right. All right. What do you want to know? I delivered the offer as I said I would."

"What'd they say?" Collins asked.

"They're going to consider it."

"What does that mean?" Brock asked.

Carrow shrugged, shook his head, and got in, slamming the door. His driver revved the engine, backed out and drove off, wheels throwing gravel.

"Gee, governor, sorry things didn't go so well," Sandusky said.

The reporters filtered back to the store's office where Antonia and the sheep ranchers still sat around the kitchen table in the back, looking in shock.

"What happened?" Brock asked Antonia. Camera lights flicked on.

Antonia squinted. "The governor delivered his offer and we are very appreciative," she answered dryly. "But we are afraid that it may not solve our problems."

"Why not?" One of the television reporters thrust a mike in her face.

"First of all, we have no way of moving our sheep to where he thinks they should go. We do not have the trucks and trailers to transport our sheep from the pastures where they are now to the pastures that Hanson has offered. It's too far to drive them on foot, especially at this time of the year. The lambs are not strong enough."

She looked at one of the older ranchers who cleared his throat. "It is not good for the sheep to be moving around all the time. They need quiet. Many lambs could die on such a trip," he said with dark, sad eyes and a weathered face.

Another lifted his hat to smooth his thin gray hair. "It was nice of the governor to come here and visit," he said, "but we do not have the money to pay what Hanson wants to charge!" He tapped a thick finger on the table, his eyes flaring. "The land we need is right here. It's our land. We want to use it. It is rightfully ours."

"Is that what you told the governor?" Jackson asked.

"This is...a very difficult situation," Antonia said stiffly, choosing her words.

"So what's next?" Brock asked.

"We promised him we would consider the offer. And we will," Aguilar said. "We will contact him when we make a decision."

"When might that be?"

Antonia shrugged. The sheep ranchers fell silent, arms resolutely folded across their chests.

"The thing you have to remember," Antonia said, "is that Carrow can solve the problem right now."

"How's that?" Brock asked.

"Tear down the fence."

※15※

Ojo Caliente

Ariel slept. The manager had agreed to let her stay in one of the spa's private casitas for a few weeks—at least until she could get back on her feet. Jackson did not want to leave her alone in her mobile home for now, and turned from his laptop to watch her. The quiet click of the keyboard had not disturbed her. Jackson looked at the empty screen that beckoned for words. He smiled to himself. The sheep ranchers had rained on the governor's parade. That was news.

> EL VALLE, N.M. – Protesting wool growers on Tuesday said thanks, but no thanks to an effort by Gov. Jack Carrow to move them and their flocks off public lands.
>
> The Hispanic sheep ranchers said they could neither afford to graze their sheep on private land, and if they did, they still lacked the necessary equipment for the move.
>
> Carrow's offer was an attempt to resolve a dispute between the state Wildlife Department and angry sheep ranchers who claim historic grazing rights to a state operated wildlife area.
>
> The ranchers and protesters are now in the second week of armed occupation of the land they say is part of a community land grant that's dates from hundreds of years earlier. The land, however, is now claimed by absentee owners by virtue of a chain of title currently on file.

Jackson stretched his arms above his head, then slumped forward, and massaged his jaw and he reviewed what he'd written. He flipped through his notebook to find a good quote to support his opening sentence. Images of the governor jumping in his car and driving away floated through his mind. "It's our land. We want to use it," one of the ranchers had said, and Jackson inserted the quote. He modemed the story by mid-afternoon, which was well in advance of the deadline, after adding a note to the bottom of the story with the telephone number of the hot springs office and his casita number. Ariel was now awake and stared at him with teary eyes.

"How are you feeling?" he asked.

Her chin quivered. "I don't know," she croaked. He went to her and she reached up to him. "I don't feel well."

"It's okay, it's okay," he said as he held her. "Try to relax. You've been through a lot."

Her body shook. She was hot, perspiring. Ariel breathed spasmodically. "Oh, my God," she cried softly, turning her head away.

Jackson held her hand, watching her with fear and confusion. There was little he could do but tell her to be calm. "Take some deep breaths. Try to relax. It's all right." She sucked in a breath, haltingly, then exhaled slowly. She inhaled again a little deeper, then coughed. "Good. Good. That's better." She took a deeper breath and exhaled. She gripped his hand with amazing strength. He released her hand, then went to the bathroom where he dampened a towel and used it to cool her forehead. She was breathing calmly now.

"What's happening to me?"

"Just relax," he said again, squeezing her hand.

She stared at the ceiling with unfocused eyes.

"Ariel, I'm going to take you to a doctor."

"No. I'm all right."

"You are not all right. Just look at you."

"I'm okay. Something just came over me. I feel better now. Really." She brushed away tears with the back of her hand. Jackson sighed. With effort she sat up, smiled weakly, and swung her legs down from the side of the bed. Walking unsteadily to the small sink, she bent and splashed water on her face. Jackson handed her a towel.

§

After convincing Ariel to join him in a hot tub at the springs, Jackson tried to relax as sweat trickled down his forehead. He sat neck-deep in the hot springs and lifted warm water to rinse his face. Eyes closed, he inhaled mineral-scented air, then glanced at Ariel, who looked at the walls, her eyes vacant. She had suffered and he was angry about and frustrated with himself because there was nearly nothing he could do about it. She had been attacked for no reason, only because she was there. Jackson's chest tightened, his heart pounded.

Ariel groaned.

He looked at her again. "Are you alright?"

"Yes."

He shook his head, dismissing her comment. "I'm very worried about you."

"I'll be all right," Ariel said, extending a hand to his shoulder. "I was just thinking of my mother. She used to give me herbal tea when I was upset. It made me sleep."

The comment made Jackson feel guilty, as if he wasn't doing enough to speed her recovery. He'd make herbal tea for her back at her home.

§

Long streaks of orange sunlight filled the sky, igniting the underside of clouds. Inside, the stucco walls of the store glowed orange. The worn, wooden floor creaked as Jackson and Ariel walked to the end of well-stocked shelves and found a wire rack of sealed, clear plastic bags, each stapled with a labeled, "*Tia Flora's Remedios*" with a rendering of an elderly woman's face.

Ariel held one to her nose and inhaled. "Hmmm." She replaced it and sorted through the other packets, picking up several, inhaling deeply with each. The herbs carried strong scents, like rich spices, and mingled with the mustiness of the store. Ariel selected a couple. "I'd like to meet this Tia Flora," she said. "Look," she said, with surprise, fingering the label. "She lives in El Valle!"

§

The scent of steaming herbs filled the casita, reminding Jackson of wet straw. Ariel poured the freshly brewed tea into a cup, and sat on the bed with crossed legs as she sipped. Jackson sat at the kitchen table staring at his lap top screen, then glanced at her. She was already asleep, curled in a fetal position, her empty teacup on the nightstand.

Jackson paced the room, then tore a page out of his notebook and scribbled a note to Ariel that he was taking her car to Santa Fe to get his mail and would return the next morning. He signed it simply "Luke." He went to the bed where Ariel was sleeping, her mouth open, a wet spot on the pillow. Jackson kissed her gently on the cheek.

The air was cool outside and the sky was still faintly light in the west, high over the mounded, rocky hills behind the spa. He made sure the door to the spa's casita was locked, then climbed into Ariel's black Saab.

§

In the darkness, Jackson drove the Saab slowly down the dirt road towards Ariel's old rental. The lights of the neighboring house were dark. Jackson cut the engine and the car lights. A three-quarter moon had risen in the south, casting a blue glow across the land. He opened the car door slowly, climbed out, then gently closed it. He felt like an intruder, but then no one was there in Ariel's mobile home to notice. The door to the small home was unlocked and he pushed it gently open and closed it behind him. Inside, he wandered from room to room, and growing more bold, turned on the lights. He opened kitchen drawers. Nothing. Under the sink and beside a pile of old rags, was a spray can of Raid, a cracked extension cord, and a small claw hammer with a wooden handle. The head rattled, but it wouldn't come off. This would do.

But no, he told himself. You can't do this. Yes you can, he said, arguing with himself as he thought again of Ariel. He took the cord, the can of Raid and the hammer to the bedroom, then went back and turned off lights. In the darkness he sat on the edge of the bed. You're crazy. Let the law handle it. No. But letting the law handle this was the same as doing nothing. Silence in the face of atrocity is wrong, he told himself. He thought of Ariel's bruised and swollen face. He felt the anger rising again. He leaned back on mattress, his left hand behind his head, his right gripping the hammer. He stared into the darkness, listening to the distant noises, car engines revving, dogs barking.

He had not meant to fall asleep, but awoke to the pounding beat of thumping rap music. He went to the mobile home's bedroom window. The neighboring lights were on, cars were parked outside. It was party time. Jackson returned to the bed and lay down. But the boom and thump reverberated through the windows, the walls, and his body. How and why Ariel put up with this was beyond him. To his mind, the sounds were hymns to abuse and violence, death knells of a dying breed. He looked at his watch. It was nearly dawn. He went to the bathroom and washed his face and dried it with his shirt tails. When he returned the sound was gone. The sky was beginning to grow light. He quietly walked to Ariel's Saab, got in, and drove away.

§

At the mailstop in Santa Fe that morning, Murray nodded a greeting while he lit a Camel with his metal Zippo, inhaling deeply. A glass ashtray on the counter was mounded with mangled butts. Murray's basketball-sized stomach strained at denim farmers overalls.

"Any mail for me?"

Murray nodded. "You been up north for a while?"

Jackson nodded. "When did you join military intelligence?"

Murray smiled and grunted. "You got a bunch of stuff here, buddy," he said walking away. He returned with two bundles, a log of rolled newspapers tied tightly with white string and a wad of letters, He set them on the counter.

"How do you tie such tight little knots with those big fingers?"

"Fine military training," he said with a cheesy grin, blowing smoke into the air. "You got a lot of crap in there from those environment groups, you know."

Jackson swallowed. His head ached from too little sleep. His eyes felt like sandpaper. He was exhausted and did not feel like hearing Murray's crap. "I like to keep tabs on what's happening. It's my business, you know."

"Them bastards is ruining this country. They're nothin' but a bunch of communists."

"I doubt it."

He handed the bundle to Jackson, looking disgusted. "Here."

Jackson cut the strings with his small pocket knife and sorted through it all. Bill Stacy, his Denver editor, had sent him editions containing his stories. He unfolded them, scanning the stories with pleasure. They were getting nice play. He sorted through the mail. There were checks from the *Herald*, too. He smiled as he cut open the envelopes. "Murray, you're a good man. Thanks."

Murray shook his head. "Don't get too close to them crazies."

§

Jackson dropped the mail and newspapers on his kitchen table. The place smelled stale and felt musty. A grease-stained, but empty pizza box sat on his coffee table. He thought about his daughter, Luna. What was she doing? He needed to give her a call. He opened a window and felt a slight breeze mingle with the still air. He crushed the pizza box and stuffed it into a trash bag that he carried outside to the metal trash can. His mobile phone rang from where he'd left it on the kitchen table. He hurried back in to get it.

"They've got Manuelito!" a panicked female voice said.

"What?"

"This is Antonia! They've taken Manuelito!" She squeaked out a cry.

"Who's taken him?"

"The police. They've arrested him."

"What for?"

"The murder of Viejo!"

"That's crazy."

"He's at the Espanola jail! Hurry!"

※16※

"Hold it right there." A beefy cop with a round face and thumbs hooked inside his holster belt blocked the doorway. Jackson showed the man his press pass. The officer held it between his fingers, looked over his shoulder at the small crowd inside, and nodded. As Jackson went to slip past, but the cop pushed him, pinning him against the door frame. Jackson glared, confused. The cop grinned, then backed off. Jackson shook his head in disgust.

The jail's reception area was bright blue painted concrete block with a swept concrete floor. Antonia sat against the wall in a plastic chair, her face drawn and gray in the florescent light. She stroked Manuelito's tousled hair, but he tilted his head away, trying to be a young man about it all. But Manuelito's wide eyes and the grim set to his mouth revealed the depth of his fear. Antonia looked at Jackson and nodded solemnly. That the state police would arrest this kid was cruel and wasteful.

A tall man with blond hair tied in a ponytail, wearing jeans and a corduroy coat, said, "Antonia," summoning her to the counter.

Despite a dozen people, mostly cops, the room was hushed except for the soft scuffle of movement. She and the man whispered. She shook her head. His whispering became more insistent. She shook her head, no. He drew back and sighed. Antonia put her hands to her face and cried and they went to Manuelito where a plain-clothed officer, badge on his belt, sat beside him. "I need a moment with my client," the lawyer said brusquely. The plain-clothed officer moved away. Antonia, Manuelito and the lawyer disappeared into a small side room and closed the door. Five minutes later only the lawyer and Antonia emerged, her eyes wet, brushing past Jackson and out the door. Jackson followed. Other press people had arrived and were out of their cars, bolstering the crowd.

"What happened?" Collins shouted. Photographers snapped frames.

The lawyer raised his hand. “My name is Richard Montrose. I’m an attorney and resident of Espanola. I represent Manuelito Aguilar.”

“The kid was arrested?” Jackson asked.

“Manuelito Aguilar has been charged with an open count of murder in connection with the death of his grandfather, Arturo Aguilar, the man known as El Viejo.”

“How old is he?”

“Eleven.”

“Why is he a suspect?”

“The police claim the boy’s fingerprints are all over a weapon found at the scene.”

“When did the shooting happen?”

“Three weeks ago. At the time, the death was ruled accidental and the old man was buried. There was no investigation. Only after the land grant protest began did the state police begin investigating.”

“Why would the kid kill his grandfather?”

“He didn’t.” Montrose waved his hand. “Look. We have to go. That’s all I can say for now.” He took Antonia by the elbow and started to walk away, then turned back. “I can tell you this. Their case is pathetic. It’s the worst police work I have ever seen.” As Montrose led Antonia away, she glumly glanced over her shoulder at Jackson. He waved weakly.

§

The young camp guard, matchstick in the corner of his mouth, sat on the tailgate and stared, then waved Jackson through. Jackson parked between two chamisa bushes and walked up the dirt road to the campfire where a man wearing a cowboy hat squatted, elbows on his knees, and smoked a hand-rolled cigarette. His stained and worn cowboy hat was pushed back on his head, revealing a smooth, bronze face and penetrating gaze. He rose warily and nodded as Jackson recognized him as the man known as Trini, short for Trinidad, from the shearing.

“I need to talk to El Cuchillo,” Jackson said. “The police have arrested the boy, Manuelito.”

Trini squinted. “Heard that.” He held his cigarette out in front of him, flicking the ash off with his little finger.

“Is El Cuchillo around?”

He nodded. The door to pale green trailer opened and El Cuchillo came out, pulling his mask down over his face. He had a military style .45-caliber pistol stuck in his pants. "This is a state of war," he blurted when he got to the fire, raising a fist.

Jackson opened his notebook and wrote down the remark. He looked at El Cuchillo, waiting for him to continue.

"The enemy has taken an innocent young man as their prisoner. It's a cheap trick." El Cuchillo looked off to the Brazos cliffs, now slate gray in the mid-day light. "This shows what kind of people we're dealing with. They use a child as a bargaining chip. They will stop at nothing." His voice grew louder. "They are cowards. They hide behind women and children. They do not have the courage to fight like men," he said. "They are less than men." He crossed his arms and spit into the fire. "They are worms."

Jackson scribbled in his notebook and flipped to a clean page. These were theatrics, but were good for his story, he thought. "Manuelito's prints were found on the weapon."

"That proves nothing! Manuelito could have been defending himself from an attack, just like the old man. Who knows?" El Cuchillo lowered his voice, then leaned toward Jackson and spoke in a whisper. "They do not know what kind of bullet killed the old man. El Viejo is buried. No autopsy was done."

"Then who killed El Viejo?"

El Cuchillo cleared his throat and spoke sternly. "We are conducting our own investigation. We cannot discuss it."

"Who's doing it?

"Trini, here," he said, gesturing. "He's been tracking prints at the scene."

Trini nodded and smiled.

"You call this a war?" Jackson asked El Cuchillo.

"The United States has waged war on brown-skinned people since the beginning. They have taken everyone's land and killed anyone who resisted. That's not war?" El Cuchillo motioned to him. "I want to show you something."

They walked past the trailer and through the shadows of the pines to the edge of the trees where El Cuchillo stepped down into a trench dug behind a low wall of green nylon sandbags. It smelled of fresh dirt and pine sap. A sleeping bag was spread on a foam pad resting on a bed made of boards and concrete blocks. Below it was a metal ammunition box and a green crate.

"We man the bunkers 'round the clock," El Cuchillo said, looking hard. "This one is Trini's." El Cuchillo squatted and unsnapped a green metal ammo box to reveal hundreds of rounds, brass casings glimmering. Snapping it shut, he pushed it back, then pulled out the crate and lifted the lid. A stubby grenade launcher was nestled on a bed of grenades like green metal baseballs. El Cuchillo hefted the grenade launcher, snapped it shut and flipped up the sight. He poked the stubby barrel out of the horizontal opening of the bunker, his knee braced against the pine logs. "Bam!" he said loudly. Jackson flinched. El Cuchillo turned and grinned. "This is a good defensive position. We have clear fields of fire." He replaced the grenade launcher, closed the lid and kicked the box back under the bunk.

"Where'd you get this stuff?"

El Cuchillo ignored the question. He rapped his knuckles on the logs. "We dug the bunkers, cut the trees. The sandbags are courtesy of the state Highway Department." He chuckled at the irony.

They climbed out and walked down a small incline along the edge of pines and aspens to another bunker. Like the first, it blended into the landscape under a covering of grass clumps and rocks. Inside a man rubbed a small, hand-held machine gun with an oily rag. He nodded slightly towards El Cuchillo, but did not look at Jackson. "This is Sixto. He's a Vietnam vet. He helped us with the bunkers." Sixto stared at his gun. Jackson recognized him as well from the shearing, but felt uneasy.

"What kind of gun is that?"

"Uzi," Sixto grunted. He slipped the Uzi's strap over his shoulder and jumped to his feet. Jackson stepped back. Sixto jerked the gun toward the log wall and squeezed the trigger. It clicked. Sixto turned slowly to Jackson and grinned widely.

"We are prepared," El Cuchillo said, squinting at Jackson to gauge his reaction. Jackson nodded, struggling to accept take it all. Prepared? They wouldn't stand a chance against a well-armed SWAT team. This place would be smoke and cinder minutes.

Back at the campfire, El Cuchillo went to a long table covered with a blue oil cloth. Iridescent green flies were at the stains and crumbs. He grabbed a gray wash rag from a nail and swiped the counter, sending the flies buzzing. "Coffee?"

Jackson nodded.

El Cuchillo handed Jackson a blue enameled cup and filled it with steaming coffee from the big pot. Jackson sipped, catching grounds on his tongue. El Cuchillo rubbed his cheek through the ski mask and looked at the sky. "It's getting hot," he said, slipping his hand under to scratch his face.

§

> EL VALLE, N.M. – An eleven-year-old boy was arrested here Tuesday and charged with the murder of his grandfather, an elderly shepherd. The arrest is the latest twist to an armed land grant protest now in its third week.
>
> The masked leader of the protest, who goes by the name of El Cuchillo, "the knife" in Spanish, called the arrest of Manuelito Aguilar, eleven years of age, an act of cowardice.
>
> "These people will stop at nothing. They are cowards. They will hide behind women and children," El Cuchillo said. The arrest of the boy escalated the protest to "a state of war," he said.

Jackson sat back in his chair at the spa hotel room, massaged his jaw for a moment, then picked up his mobile phone and called state police headquarters. "Vince Taylor, please." He waited until Taylor came on. "It's Luke Jackson. I'm up north here with the land grant protesters. What can you tell me about the arrest of the kid, Manuelito Aguilar?"

"Who's that?"

"Com'on, Vince. The eleven-year-old kid, charged with murder."

"Oh, yeah."

"You guys would do that to a kid?"

"Of course. He knows how to use a gun. Every boy up there does. They grow up with them."

"That's a quote?"

"Ahhh, no. Look, the kid's prints were all over it. He's the only one we can place at the scene near the old man's time of death."

"What's the motive?"

"I'm not a mind reader."

"El Cuchillo says this is a war now."

"You're going to write that?"

"Are you guys going to move against the camp?"

"You think I'm going to tell you?" Taylor paused. "All I can say is that we are prepared to enforce the law."

"Good, Vince. We all can sleep easy tonight. So you're prepared to storm the place?"

"I didn't say that."

"The dogs are drooling, aren't they."

Taylor cleared his throat. "We have a specialized, highly-trained and heavily-equipped unit that can be put in place anywhere in the state of New Mexico in a matter of hours. Our primary goal is to keep the peace and insure the safety of everyone in the state."

"Which means?"

"Jesus Christ, Jackson." The phone clicked and the call ended.

Jackson held the phone at arm's length, then he put it in his pocket. Things were escalating faster than he had anticipated.

The door to the room opened and light streamed in, silhouetting Ariel.

"Hi," Jackson said. "How are you?"

"Where'd you go?"

"I left you a note."

"But you took my car."

"Was that all right?"

"You didn't ask." Ariel closed the door slowly. "But that's all right. It's not as though I needed it. She went to Jackson and gently massaged his shoulders.

"Feels good," Jackson said softly. He had had little sleep in the past twenty-four hours and his back and shoulders ached.

"What are you writing?" She rested a hand on his shoulder and put her face next to his to view the screen. Her touch was soft and warm.

"They arrested a young boy, accused him of murdering an old man, the shepherd who was found dead."

"That's awful," she said, slipping a hand to the top button of his shirt, loosening it, and touching his chest.

Jackson sighed. "I have to finish this story."

"I know," she whispered, then gently kissed his neck.

"Please, Ariel."

"Aaugh," she said, turning and throwing herself onto the short couch. She put an arm behind her head and glared.

“Ariel, you’ve been through a lot. It’s not time.”

A thick silence hung in the air. “What do you know?”

Jackson looked her. “I need to finish this. Please.”

Her face began to break, tears brimming in her eyes. He went to her, bent and tried to hold her, but she pushed him away. He felt like a father, suddenly older, acutely aware of their age difference. This wouldn’t work, he thought. She turned away.

※17※

Santa Fe

"It'll be a few minutes," the clerk in the Elections Bureau said. "You can't take them out of the office."

"I know." Jackson followed her through a maze of cubicles in office on the top floor of the state capitol building to a long, polished wood table. Two young women behind him giggled over a photo on a cell phone.

The clerk put two thick piles of bound documents on the table with a thump. "Governor Carrow's contributions are here," she said, palm on one stack. "Expenditures are here," palm on the other. "Ten cents a page for copies."

"I'm with the press."

"Ten cents a page." She had a drawn, tired face. She limped away on swollen ankles.

When Jackson left the Election Bureau two hours later, he had what he needed.

Down the curving hallway, he stopped at the state Finance Committee office and asked the receptionist for the committee's chief of staff, Pablo Ramirez.

"He's not in," she said. Bright red lipstick covered thick, pouty lips and curled black hair fell on the shoulders of her blue satin blouse.

"Who's overseeing the state Wildlife Department budget these days?"

She looked over his shoulder. "Let me see." She dialed a number. "Marsha, someone here wants to talk about the Wildlife Department." After a few moments, she looked at him and pointed a finger down the hall. "First office on your right."

The placard by the door read Marsha Stone. When he pushed open the door, she looked up from her desk. "Luke Jackson. What you been up to?"

"Same old stuff."

She ran her fingers through shoulder-length brown hair, then came from behind her desk to clear a stack of papers off a padded chair so he could sit. A stout mountain bike with knobby tires rested against the wall below a poster of red rock cliffs and the word MOAB in big block letters.

"Moab. Nice spot, huh?"

She smiled. "Awww. I love it there."

Jackson nodded. "What can you tell me about the Johnson Wildlife Area up there in Rio Arriba County?"

"Off the record?"

"Sure."

"They arrested someone up there, didn't they?"

"A kid."

She shook her head, then adjusted her denim skirt as she pulled a fat three-ring binder from the shelf. "I remember something about that," she said fanning through pages. She stopped at a page, ran a finger down it, then flipped to the next. "Okay. Here. This was last year's budget." She came around the desk and pointed to a number which Jackson wrote down. "Now here," she said, taking another book from the shelf, "is this year's." She found the right page quickly and pointed. "There's hardly any difference."

"Don't they have any specific appropriations for projects?"

She shook her head. "No, not really. Each category, like wildlife management or law enforcement, gets an appropriation, but they spend it how they want."

"Nothing specific?"

She wrinkled her forehead. "Now that you mention it." She went to the shelf and pulled out a thinner document. "Remember that supplemental appropriations bill they passed in the closing minutes of the last session? It had lots of goodies. Each line item was a specific appropriation to a legislator's pet project." She flipped through pages. "Here. Look at this. A hundred fifty thousand dollars, Johnson Wildlife Area. Fencing and security."

Jackson wrote down the figures. "Who sponsored the bill?"

"It was a committee substitute for dozens of bills wrapped into one." She showed him the cover page that listed all the bill numbers. Jackson thumbed through the legislative bill directory and found House Bill 898, sponsored by Representative Henry Zamora, a Democrat from Española. The bill had been introduced late, real late in the session, but had sailed through two committees and was included in the final version of the supplemental appropriations bill. Jackson knew Zamora. He ran a successful car repair business and travel station. He had been a deputy sheriff and then was elected county sheriff. Now he was a state representative.

He read from the bill: "Due to extensive poaching resulting in the degradation and depletion of wildlife; and, due to the commitment by the State of New Mexico to the preservation and enhancement of wildlife, the sum of $150,000 is appropriated for the care and maintenance of elk herds in the Johnson Wildlife Area."

Jackson called Zamora's garage to get a comment. A woman answered. "Zamora Exxon."

"Is Henry Zamora in?"

"Who's calling, please?"

"Luke Jackson. I'm a reporter with *The New Mexican* newspaper." He could hear people talking in the background, the sound of cars coming and going, the clang of a bell and, close by, the woman yelling to Zamora that a reporter was on the phone.

"This is Henry."

Jackson explained that he was working on a story about the Johnson Wildlife Area. He wanted to know how the bill had come about.

"Someone asked me to introduce it," Zamora said.

"Someone? Who?"

"That lobbyist. The big guy. Norton. The one with the handlebar mustaches."

"Frank Norton?"

"Yeah, that's him."

"Did he say why?"

"He said it would help the elk. I'm a big supporter of wildlife."

"Henry, thanks a lot." Jackson hung up, tapping a few beats on his notebook with a pen.

§

Frank Norton stared into his tumbler of Jack Daniels with light blue eyes set under thick, reddish-gray eyebrows. Large, pale hands cupped the glass. "It's a casual kind of thing," he said with a deep voice. "Carl Hanson and I have been friends since we attended the New Mexico Military Institute together." He looked across the restaurant, momentarily lost in the memory. "God that was long ago!" he said, snapping back. "Class of nineteen sixty-five!" He lifted his right hand, showed the class ring on his finger. Norton shrugged, as if it was insignificant. "I do him a favor once in a while and he invites me hunting up there every fall. It's great. Do you hunt?"

Jackson smiled. "In a manner of speaking."

"Hah," Norton blurted. "You hunt for them big stories, do ya?" He elbowed a woman sitting next to him with black hair and wearing a burnt orange suit jacket and dress. She smiled politely at Jackson, then winked as she sipped white wine. The look told him she tolerated Norton with bemused boredom.

"Since Frank isn't going to introduce us...." She extended her delicate hand across the table. "I'm Anita Moreno."

"Oh, I thought you knew each other," Norton said apologetically.

"Didn't you used to work for Senator Rogers?" Jackson asked.

She nodded. "A while back. I joined Frank's lobbying firm as an associate about a year ago."

Jackson smiled and looked at Norton. "Adding a touch of class, I see."

Norton cleared his throat. "So, are you hungry?"

"Sure."

Norton waved at a waitress, ordered more drinks and the special of the day, grilled salmon. "Got to watch my waist," he said, slapping his girth.

Moreno smiled politely.

Jackson ordered iced tea and a cheese burger, but suddenly felt conspicuous sitting there with the man. Norton and other big lobbyists had standing reservations there for lunch. Everyone could see who was talking to whom.

"So you and Hanson go way back?"

Norton nodded. "Yeah. We were in Vietnam together, too. Hanson was decorated. Two tours. Made captain real fast. He was a major when he was drummed out."

Jackson stared at Norton. "Drummed out?"

Norton furrowed his brow. "Bad choice of words. He resigned. Career military takes a certain kind of person. Hanson was too independent. He's not the kind of guy who puts up with a lot of bullshit." He paused. "A lot of us knew how to win that war if the top brass would have let us. But they didn't wanna win. Can you believe it?" Norton's raised and lowered his eyebrows. "That war was not about fighting communism. The only trouble is that me and Hanson didn't figger that out until it was too late."

"Too late? Too late for what?"

"To late to make some money, that's what." Norton slurped his drink. "We were over there at the same time, but we didn't see each other much. But that's all history now. Say, what are you working on?"

Jackson shrugged. "This land grant protest up in El Valle."

"Those people better be careful. You too. They're really stirring up a hornet's nest."

"Well, they have a good claim."

"Shit. It's a land grab, pure and simple."

"I don't know."

"A word of advice. When someone pulls the trigger, you better duck."

※18※

Santa Fe

At five twenty-five Jackson turned down Spruce Street, stopping at a one-story, ranch-style house with pale brown stucco in one of Santa Fe's post-WWII neighborhoods. It was the house he and Margo had purchased ten years earlier, before Luna came along, before they fell out of love, before everything. He turned off the engine, closed his eyes, and mentally went through the house, remembering the kitchen cabinets had been painted orange and that the plants they had put into the house a few days before the furniture arrived had dropped their leaves because the landlord left the doors open in January to let the new paint to dry. He remembered their dog Annie, the Australian shepherd had a litter of pups under their bed and kept them up all night.

He opened his eyes to the sound of tapping on his car window. It was Luna, her nose mashed against the passenger window, grinning. He smiled and nodded and she yanked the door open, climbed in, and wrapped her sinewy arms around his neck, hugging him tightly.

§

Tomasita's restaurant was crowded inside so they were seated on the patio. The sun was low in the sky, the patio bathed in deep yellow light. Jackson put on his sunglasses and ordered a margarita and a cherry coke for Luna. She had brown hair pulled back into a French twist, exposing her high forehead and freckled face and nose. He noticed a small ring pierced in her left ear lobe.

"When'd you get that?" he asked, fingering it.

"The other day."

"Like it?"

She nodded.

“Margo says you’re going to be a tennis player.”

“I learned already,” she said. “Mommy and Jim say I’m real good and the camp is nice.”

“Are you ready for three weeks of tennis this summer?”

“There’s lots of other things to do besides tennis. It’s by a big, famous lake. There’s boating and swimming. Horses and stuff.”

“Lake Tahoe.”

“Yeah. Something like that.”

“Who’s paying for it?”

“Jim. He says I’ll have a lot of fun.”

“It’s a long way away.”

She shrugged and looked away.

“May I take your order?” asked a puffy-faced waitress who squinted against the sun.

§

After dinner, he drove the short distance and parked in a public garage near the Plaza. They walked up San Francisco Street to the Haagen-Dazs ice cream store, dodging meandering tourists. Gangly boys with Rastafarian hair crowded around the entrance. Barrel-like shorts, T-shirts printed with marijuana leaves and floppy tennis shoes completed the uniform. Teenage girls with pierced noses, lips, eyebrows, and belly buttons had pink eye shadow and purple hair. His hand protectively on her shoulder, Jackson steered Luna past the teenagers to the high glass counter. They meandered the length of it, mesmerized by the myriad of flavors in the containers filling the cooler behind and below the sloping window.

“Decide yet?” said a young clerk with a clean-cut and smiling face.

Jackson looked down at Luna. “Know what you want?”

“Chocolate.”

“And you, sir?”

“Vanilla with chocolate chips and almonds.”

Ice cream cups in hand, they crossed to the Plaza and sat on the curved stone bench surrounding the monument where once a stone obelisk stood tall. On a hot day in August, 1974, the word “savage,” which had been used to describe the local pueblo Indian natives who had been confronted by the Union soldiers in the area, had been chiseled off.

As he sat, Jackson felt desperately lonely, like he was losing her, like she was already gone. His daughter was growing up without him. She was going off to California for three weeks and Margo had only mentioned it in passing, as if it didn't matter that he knew or not. It had already been decided. Anger burned in him. But maybe, he thought, it was for the best. He put his arm around Luna and she leaned her head against him. He wanted to sit there with her forever.

"You're not going to become one of those, are you?"

Luna lifted her big blue eyes. "What?"

"Plaza rats."

"Yeech," she said, curling her nose in disgust.

A high-rider truck revved its engine and rumbled around the Plaza. A bright red Nissan sedan with trunk open and small gold-spoked wheels boomed loudly, giant bass speakers vibrating the air, drowning out all other sounds. The deep thumping made his stomach ache.

§

Later that day, her skinny arms wrapped around his neck, he hugged her tight.

"Com'on, sweety. You have to go now." She relaxed and he let her go, noticing her tears. "Go see your mother now."

Margo stood in the doorway, partially hidden by the screen, watching. He blinked his own eyes. His throat felt thick. Luna paused at the door and gave him a small wave before disappearing inside.

※19※

Santa Fe

The high sun pounded the pavement. Heat waves shimmered from the dirt hills in the distance. A dust devil swirled and danced, scattering twigs and brush. Like everyone else, Jackson turned a shoulder to it and covered his eyes. A camera man cursed, shielding his equipment with his body. He brushed away grit in the ensuing calm. Manuelito's arraignment in the small courtroom beside the jail was scheduled for ten o'clock. It was ten-thirty. Since he was a juvenile, cameras were banned from the courtroom, but Manuelito had to cross on the sidewalk from the jail to the courthouse. Deputies and the press waited in the opening.

Jackson stood back from crowd and leaned against his truck, watching. A bead of sweat dripped down his temple. He pulled off his sunglasses and wiped the lenses with his shirttail. A half-dozen crows circled above, casting shadows on the gathered crowd. He sighed, crossed his arms and watched the birds, then dropped his gaze to a pair of black beetles scuttling across the pavement, animated by the heat, one on top of the other.

"Could get hot today," Jackson said.

"Hmmm," Collins moaned, looking across the empty space. His eyes widened as he noticed movement. "Looks like something's happening."

Deputies straightened, hands on weapons. The door opened and two plain-clothed officers emerged, followed by Montrose and a tall, heavyset officer. Through the lenses, the cameramen followed their approach. The officer held a sheet of paper, stopped near the press and read from it.

"There will be no arraignment today of Manuelito Aguilar," he said brusquely. He exhaled heavily. "At approximately four-fifteen today, several masked and armed men entered the Espanola Municipal Detention Facility and demanded the release of a juvenile prisoner, Manuelito Aguilar. The guard on duty, fearing for his life, released the prisoner. That is all I can say now," he said gruffly. The television cameras rolled. The 35-mms clicked. He turned to leave.

"Who are you?" one of the cameramen barked at the announcing officer.

"I'm Edward Ulibarri, the Espanola Chief of Police." He walked away.

Montrose stayed.

"Was anyone injured?" Collins asked.

Montrose shook his head. "I don't know a lot of the details, but as far as I know, no one was hurt."

"Who sprung him?" Jackson asked.

"Guess," he said, grinning.

"Didn't any alarms go off?" Collins asked.

"Apparently the alarm system didn't work. It may have turned off."

"Does that mean it was an inside job?" Jackson asked.

"We have no further comment," Montrose said.

Collins glanced at Jackson and grinned. "This is great. Just great."

"Son of a bitch," Jackson said, doing a little dance. He nervously fumbled for his cell phone and dialed the newspaper office. The regional editor, Bill Stacy, would love this. He knew now that he needed to go north again to the camp. He spun his tires pulling onto the highway headed north, his mind brimming, and called in the story as he drove.

§

Less than a hour later, a patrolman stopped him at a yellow tape police barrier at the cattle guard entrance to the camp. Police squad cars and a couple of television station vans were parked at the side of the road nearby. Jackson held out his press pass.

"Sorry, this is as far as you go."

"I need to get up there."

"Sorry." The cop wore aviator sunglasses and a motorcycle helmet with a short visor.

Jackson watched a police helicopter make low, but wide circles over the camp. High overhead a fixed-wing airplane droned. Suddenly, three state squad cars appeared, and once the tape was moved, they bounced up the dirt road, undercarriages scraping. He spotted Vince Taylor, the state police spokesman, in the trailing car and the state police chief in the other.

Collins and Brock came up behind him.

"What's going on?" Collins asked.

"Nothing yet. Taylor and Chief Woodward just went by."

An hour passed. It was eerily quiet. The calm was broken by a small helicopter thudding toward them high over the road. It swooped skyward at a sharp angle, then banked to the right and came down a hundred yards away and settled on a dirt road nearby, blowing dust and dirt. "Action Eight" was blazed across the side in bright, blue letters with a large numeral 8 inside a circle.

The engine whined and slowly died. A man wearing a tan safari jacket jumped out, followed by a soundman, camera man, and light man. The jacketed correspondent ran up to the state patrolman. "Where's the camp?"

The patrolmen calmly pointed a thumb over his shoulder.

"That's it?"

The patrolman nodded.

"Can we get there?"

The patrolman shook his head. "No."

"Look, I'm, Rodrick Goodman of Channel Eight. We'd like to interview the protesters."

"Sorry."

Goodman scowled, turned to his crew, scanned the area, then pointed. "Let's set up over there. We have to go live in thirty minutes." He turned to the cop. "Where's the chief? We need to talk to him. Whose truck is this? We need it moved."

"Mine," Jackson said.

"Could you move it?"

"Anything for Channel Eight."

Goodman scrambled toward the tape line, waving to his crew to follow. Jackson put his truck in gear, spun the tires, spewing dirt on Goodman. He glared at Jackson and brushed his pant leg.

Jackson sat in his truck, opened his laptop, which sprang to life, and began to type.

ESPANOLA, N.M. – Masked gunmen entered the jail here in the early morning hours Thursday and kidnapped an eleven-year-old boy who was to be arraigned on murder charges.

Police suspect the kidnappers are part of a land grant protest that began three weeks ago over claims that a state wildlife area was illegally transferred to the government more than 100 years ago.

Police have surrounded an armed encampment on the disputed land near the northern New Mexico community of El Valle.

An hour later, Jackson's cell phone rang. "Hello?"

"Jackson. It's Vince Taylor."

"Vince? What's up?"

"Who's out there?"

"Collins, and Brock, Martinez, the usual crew. A couple of TV stations. Goodman's here. So's Channel Five."

"Okay. Ah, look. It's pretty complicated."

"Life is complicated, Vince. We need some information out here."

"Would you listen a minute? I need your help."

"You need my help?"

"El Cuchillo wants to issue a statement to the press."

"Great."

"But he will only give it to you."

"Why me?"

"Says he trusts you."

Jackson thought for a moment. His stomach tightened. He wanted this story badly, but he did not want to be the story. It could be a trap. Damn, he thought.

"Jackson, you there?"

"Yeah. I have to think about it for a minute."

"Now, Jackson. He wants to see you now."

Jackson's heart raced. "What if we won't let me go."

Taylor paused. "It's a risk you take."

"That's comforting, Vince." Jackson said. *Shit!* El Cuchillo wouldn't hold him, he told himself. Not now, anyway. He was already in enough trouble. El Cuchillo wanted out of this situation gracefully, if that was possible. And, Antonia was there. She'd keep things calm. "Okay," Jackson said. "What do I need to do?"

"Just come over to us. We'll explain."

Jackson clicked off. Heat waves rose in the distance, rippling the light. He went over to Brock's car, tapped on the window, and told her what he was going to do. "Sure you want to do that?" Brock said.

"It must be my fifteen minutes of fame."

The helmeted motorcycle cop, his knee-high boots coated with dust, strode over to Jackson, then motioned for him to go. Police vehicles were scattered along the road. A dozen state patrolmen stood protectively behind their cars, shotguns aimed at the camp.

Jackson nodded and walked up the road to the police line. He was nervous.

Taylor waved, his face twisted with worry. "Thanks for doin' this," he said, trying to sound friendly. They walked to the large police van, the open side door revealing an interior filled with communications equipment and television screens. Inside Tom Woodward, the state police chief, sat on a stool and leaned forward with earphones on. "Yes sir, yes sir," Woodward said. "We'll keep you posted."

"Carrow?" Jackson asked.

Woodward turned and nodded, then pulled off the headphones. His eyes were obscured behind aviator sunglasses. He ran his hand over his blond crewcut. "You're Jackson?" Jackson nodded. "Okay. We need your help. El Cuchillo wants to make a statement."

"I know."

"I want you to keep your eyes peeled, take note of what's where, especially how many and what kind of weapons they have. When you get back, you de-brief. Got it?"

Jackson swallowed. "I agreed to get a statement and come back out. I'm not going to set them up."

Woodward laughed, then coughed. "You've got to be our eyes and ears or you're going back out there with the others," he said angrily. His thin lips tightened.

Jackson stared, frozen with indecision.

"Who's side you on?"

"I don't want to see anyone killed, that's all."

"Well, if those bastards...." Woodward caught himself. "This is out of your hands. Get used to it." Woodward stared.

Jackson stared back, his heart pounding. "Okay. Tell him I'm coming."

Woodward reached for his phone and dialed. "He's comin' in." He clicked off, and sizing up Jackson, and said, "We're counting on you." Jackson looked at him and shook his head in disgust.

The posters on the gateposts fluttered in the breeze. Shouts came from the camp as Jackson walked slowly up the road in the hot sun. It was eerily quiet. *How am I supposed to do this?* He lifted his hands slightly to his sides, palms out, his long, thin reporter's notebook jammed in his back pocket. One idiot move could do him in, Jackson realized. His legs felt weak. A couple of gunmen lay flat on the ground behind trees near the campfire, their rifles pointed at him. *Where'd these people come from?* He paused as he approached the campfire, turning back to look at the police.

The door of the green trailer clicked open. A hand waved at him.

Jackson climbed the metal lath steps.

Inside, the trailer was hot and stuffy. Jackson stood in the doorway.

Antonia looked at him with wild eyes, then to El Cuchillo, who was seated at the small kitchen table. They looked like they'd been arguing. The air was thick with tension.

"How's Manuelito?" Jackson asked.

"He's here and he's fine, now that he's out of jail," Antonia said, not looking at him.

El Cuchillo motioned for Jackson to sit down at the table across from him.

Jackson slipped into the narrow seat and put his notebook on the table.

El Cuchillo flexed his hands. His eyes darted from Jackson to the window, to Antonia and back. Ski mask on, he looked at Jackson, then at the notebook. A cellular phone lay on the wooden table.

"You want to issue a statement?"

El Cuchillo nodded, cleared his throat. "We, *El Cooperativo del Valle,* have resorted to this drastic action to protect an innocent victim from the American kangaroo courts."

"Go slowly." Jackson said, writing as quickly as he could.

"A young member of our camp, Manuelito Aguilar, was falsely and stupidly accused of a crime he was incapable of committing. To charge a young man with the murder of his grandfather, the most respected elder of this community, is an outrage."

"Slow down," Jackson said again.

El Cuchillo waited for Jackson. “This is just another example of American oppression of brown-skinned people.” He paused, looked at Jackson, then Antonia.

She lowered her gaze to the floor. She didn’t look happy.

“Meanwhile, the true criminals run free,” El Cuchillo continued. “We refuse to be the victims of the white man’s atrocities. We will fight to the death to remain free.” He paused.

Jackson scribbled to catch up. “That’s it?”

“Read it back.” El Cuchillo looked out the window as Jackson read what he had written. When Jackson finished, El Cuchillo waved his hand, ending the conversation.

“One more thing,” Jackson said. “What’s your phone number?”

El Cuchillo reached for Jackson’s notebook and pen and carefully wrote the number. He gestured for Jackson to get out.

Just like that, Jackson thought. *I’m your messenger boy now.* Don’t complain, buddy, he told himself. Just get up and walk out.

Outside, the camp was quiet. The nearby world was holding its breath, Jackson thought. The fire pit smoldered, smoke swirling around the Mexican national flag fluttering atop a tall, wooden pole. Beyond, the police waited. Jackson walked slowly toward them.

※20※

Tierra Amarilla

Jackson crudely sketched the camp on a yellow legal pad, unable to shake the feeling that he was being used, by both the police and El Cuchillo. Finished, he handed the sheet to Woodward. "There's nothing there that you can't see already."

The camp was only about twenty-five yards across, centered in a clump of pines and aspens, with shallow bunkers at the edge of the tree line. The trees were dense enough to prevent the SWAT team from dropping into the middle of it from the sky. Bunkers also protected the rear. A frontal assault could be easily seen.

"Any weapons in the trailer?" Woodward asked.

"Didn't see any, other than the Uzi and the grenade launcher in the bunker."

Woodward stared. "Nothin' in the trailer?"

Jackson shook his head. "I didn't see any."

"Probably out of sight."

Jackson bit his lower lip. Woodward wanted to gauge the danger he and his men confronted. It was a clean standoff, Jackson thought. No one was going anywhere.

"God dammit," Woodward said, pulling off his sunglasses, massaging the bridge of his nose.

"Chief, we need to talk to the press now," Taylor said. "Goodman's calling for you."

Woodward turned away, head bent, as if he had not heard, then he swung around. "Okay. Let's do it."

Jackson followed the officers to the police line where Woodward got out and walked up to Goodman and shook hands.

"Can you stand over here?" Goodman said, leading the chief by the elbow. “That’s great. Yeah, that’s perfect.” Goodman’s cameraman nodded. The Channel Five cameras set up quickly beside Channel Eight’s.

Jackson, Brock, Collins, and Martinez stood back, but close enough to hear.

“Tell us what the situation is.” Goodman said, thrusting the microphone toward Woodward’s face.

Woodward cleared his throat, took off his sunglasses, and scowled. “Earlier today a young man was kidnapped at gunpoint from the Espanola Municipal Detention Center. We have reason to believe he is being held at that camp,” he said, motioning behind him.

“So now what?” Goodman said.

“We want the young man released so the court system can do its work.”

“What charges do the people here face?”

“That’s to be determined by the prosecutor, not me. But, I would guess that murder, kidnapping, assault on a police officer, escape, and conspiracy would be among them. That’s a few I can think of right now, but there’s probably more.”

“And if they won’t turn the boy over?”

“We have options.”

“Such as?”

“It wouldn’t be prudent for me to say, now would it?”

“Have you been in contact with the protest’s leader?

“Hell yes! That son-of-a....” Woodward caught himself, flashed a sheepish grin, then cleared his throat. “We are in constant communication.”

“Thanks, chief.”

Woodward nodded. “Oh, wait a minute. El Cuchillo issued a statement.” He turned to Jackson and waved a finger. “Com’ere.”

Jackson squinted, as all eyes were on him. The cameras swiveled and focused on him. Jackson’s chest tightened. Damn, he thought, I’m giving Goodman and the others some prime time visuals.

“You have a statement?” Goodman barked.

Jackson glared. “Yeah. El Cuchillo dictated it to me. It’s short.” Jackson flipped through the pages of his notebook, then looked at the cameras.

“Stand over here,” Goodman said.

"No," Jackson said. "I'm just going to read this thing."

Goodman motioned to his cameraman to keep rolling.

Jackson scowled.

§

"We're right on deadline for the regional edition," Stacy told him. "Where the hell have you been?"

"Sorry, the news doesn't happen on your schedule," Jackson said.

"Unless you file soon, we'll have to go with what AP puts out. I bent over backwards to get your story on the front page. Come through for me, okay."

"El Cuchillo called me into the camp and gave me a statement."

"Got an exclusive?"

"No. I had to share it."

"Damn."

"Part of the deal. The good news is that El Cuchillo trusts me. I can probably get back in there when I need to."

"Let's talk about it later."

§

Jackson needed an escape, and despite his deep reservations about leaving the scene, he drove the hour it took to travel to the Ojo Caliente spa. And, he badly wanted to see Ariel.

He wheeled into the hot springs, slid to a stop in front of Ariel's casita and hurried inside. Ariel was asleep on the couch. She lifted her head, opened her eyes and tried to focus. "Oh, it's you," she mumbled.

Jackson turned on the television, clunked his laptop on the table, powered up, and began to type. Using the remote, he clicked to Channel Eight. It was just six o'clock. The co-anchor, a woman, talked. The words, SPECIAL REPORT, appeared on the screen which showed Goodman at the edge of the road with the encampment in the background.

"This is where land grant protesters remained today after a daring, pre-dawn raid on the Espanola city jail from which they took a young man accused of murdering an elderly shepherd. The suspects in this bizarre kidnapping remain holed up in the forested area just behind me," Goodman said. The video cut to the Ulibarri press conference earlier in the day on the lawn of the jail in Espanola. Goodman's face again filled the screen followed by a short clip of Woodward talking. "But the protesters have not been silent," he said. "In a statement given to one of the reporters here covering the protest, the band's leader, a masked man who goes by the name of El Cuchillo, said his group would not give up without a fight." Jackson saw himself on television reading the statement.

"Damn," Jackson mumbled.

Ariel turned to him. "That' you!" she said excitedly. "You were on television!" She sat up, hugging a pillow, and smiled. "That's neat!"

Jackson shrugged and began to type.

Ariel walked over to him and slipped her arms around his shoulders. "Congratulations."

Jackson looked up at her, kissed her quickly, then unwrapped her arms from around him. "I have to write this. I'm past deadline."

"You're always grumpy," she said with a pout, turned and sat back on the couch.

Jackson shook his head and typed quickly.

※21※

Ojo Caliente

Ariel rose, found her purse, and fumbled through it for out a neatly-wound joint. She struck a match and inhaled, the acrid scent of marijuana smoke filling the room.

"Ariel, I'm sorry. I'm up against a deadline. Please."

She crossed her arms, the joint smoldering from between the tips of two fingers. He scowled.

"Why are you smoking that?"

She shrugged, took a deep drag, coughed slightly and exhaled slowly, defiantly blowing smoke through puckered lips. She went past him and stepped outside the casita door where she took another drag.

Jackson stood at the door and said, "Ariel, please."

Ignoring him, she held the joint to her lips, took another inhale, and let the smoke dribble from her mouth and nose before she walked away.

"Shit." He wanted to smoke too, but instead shook his head and returned to his story. Thirty minutes later, he called Stacy to say he'd filed his story.

Jackson picked up a pillow, flopped onto the couch cushions, and hugged it as he stared at the ceiling. His stomach ached and so did his head. He didn't know what to do about Ariel. He liked her. She was attractive and he wanted her. But she was still hurting from her assault. He wanted to make love, but felt guilty about that, as if he was enjoying the benefits of a relationship without a commitment. But maybe she needed to be loved. We all need that, he thought. We never get enough. She was no kid. She'd been around. She knew the score. If he treated like a child, that's how she'd act. He dismissed his thoughts as hunger pains told him to eat, reminding him that he had to take care of himself.

He went to the spa restaurant. It was nearly empty. Ariel sat at a corner table. When she saw him, she turned away.

"May I join you?" he asked indignantly.

She said nothing, so he sat down.

"Ariel, this story has gotten to be a pretty big deal. It's front page news. It's good for me. I can't afford to blow this opportunity. Try to understand."

"I know what your priorities are," she said sarcastically. She looked at him, as if he was treating her stupidly.

News was a drug and he was an addict. He knew it. He would go anywhere, anytime to get a good story "It's my life, Ariel."

She put her fork down, wiped her mouth, and turned away. Her eyes watered.

§

After dinner they walked back to the casita in the evening light. It was warm and for the first time in days, Jackson felt good. He took Ariel's hand, and she looked at him tentatively, then smiled and leaned against him. She slipped her arm around his waist. He stopped and looked sadly into her eyes. He bent and kissed her. She pressed up against him and wrapped her arms around him. Inside the casita, he closed the door tightly, reached for her and kissed her again, deeply.

His telephone jangled, breaking the calm. It rang five times as he debated to pick it up, but did and said, "Hello."

"Jackson? This Stacy. I'm editing your story. Got a couple questions."

"Okay."

"Why didn't the alarm system at the Espanola jail work?"

"Don't know."

"Was it checked earlier?"

"Don't know."

"Who was the guard on duty?"

"Don't know that either."

"Are you sure that is how you spell Ulibarri?"

"Yes."

"What kind of guns did they have?

"No one said."

"What does El Cuchillo mean?"

"The knife."

"What's his real name?"

"I don't know."

Malcomb sighed deeply. "That's the kind of thing you should know. Where's he from?"

"Here, I guess."

"You should know this stuff," he said. "This is really sloppy reporting. I can't believe we're running this out front."

"Look," Jackson said angrily. "This is not a personality profile. This is a story about the kidnapping of a child that's grown out of a land grant protest that's turned violent. It doesn't matter what El Cuchillo's real name is."

"Did you even bother to ask if El Cuchillo has a real name?"

"Not yet."

"Call him."

"What?"

"Call him and ask him right now."

"No."

"You have his number, don't you?"

"Of course." Jackson groaned. "I'll call you back."

His heart pounded. Dammit, he thought. He looked at Ariel and had almost forgotten that she was in the room. "Shit." His night was ruined. He flipped through his notebook to El Cuchillo's cellular phone number. A woman answered. "Antonia?"

"Yes," she said softly.

"This is Jackson."

"Where are you?"

"At the hot springs. What's going on?"

"You should be here."

"Why?"

"We cut a deal. Montrose is talking with Chief Woodward."

"Where's El Cuchillo?"

"Out in the camp. Talkin' to people, I guess. Look. I gotta go. I thought you were Montrose." She hung up.

Jackson looked at Ariel. "Gotta go," he said.

She frowned and turned away.

§

The night was dark and Jackson drove quickly, the moonlight bursting out from behind roiling black clouds, spreading a dim blue glow across the fields lining the highway. At the camp, Jackson saw the black shapes of assault helicopters sitting like giant beasts on the fields nearby. He jammed on his brakes and pulled to the side of the road, and rolled down his window to look. A generator hummed. Three helicopters waited, their long rotator blades drooping like tired wings. Men in puffy fatigues hustled about, carrying black weapons and wearing black faces. Jackson drove past the taped police line and parked among a dozen dusty police vehicles. The police had erected flood lights. Brock was already there at the command post, along with the rest of the press.

Taylor came up to him. "The SWAT team is poised to drop in there at a moment's notice. Tear gas, guns blazing. The floodlights the television guys have erected will make it easy as hell to see." He grinned nervously.

Brock leaned against the hood of the van, sipping coffee. She nodded at Jackson.

"Evenin'," she said.

"You been here all along?"

Brock nodded. "Woodward and Montrose are in the van negotiating a deal with El Cuchillo. Won't be too soon for me."

"Yeah. Did you file from here?"

"I'm phoning stuff in," Brock said. "If they hurry, Woodward can be on the 10 o'clock news, too."

"News from New Mexico."

Brock sipped her coffee. "Aaah. This tastes so bad."

The van doors opened. Woodward and Montrose stepped out. Jackson looked at Montrose. "You ready?"

Montrose nodded.

"What's up?" Brock asked.

The pony-tailed Montrose winked at her through wire rimmed glasses. "It's over."

"Aww, this was just beginning get good!" Jackson said.

Montrose shook his head in disgust.

Woodward picked up a bullhorn and strode to the entrance. "We're ready." His voice echoed over the humming generators. "Turn down those lights."

The television lights were dimmed. For a few minutes, nothing happened as the door of the green trailer opened slightly, then flew open, banging against the side. Antonia appeared in the doorway, shielding her eyes against the lights with her hand. She stopped at the bottom of the steps, turned and held out her hand to the doorway. Manuelito stepped out, and cautiously they walked past the cold campfire and down the road toward the waiting police. At the gate, Montrose took Manuelito's elbow and went to a waiting cruiser. They got in, closed the doors, and the cruiser passed the cameras and press and disappeared into the darkness.

※22※

Santa Fe

Deputies from Santa Fe and Rio Chama County Sheriff offices were posted at corners outside the Santa Fe County Courthouse. Jackson checked his watch under the shade of a towering elm: one-thirty. The sun was again high and hot. He went inside, passed by two state patrolmen, and emptied his pockets at the courthouse metal detector. A one-armed deputy, an empty sleeve pinned to his shoulder, picked up Jackson's small Swiss army knife. "Sorry, no weapons."

"That's just a penknife."

The guard shook his head. "We had a lawyer get cut by one of those things. Claim it on your way out."

More deputies leaned against the wrought iron railing that surrounded the upper floor balcony. From behind the glass walls of the court clerk's office, secretaries watched. Another officer checked Jackson's ID before he entered the courtroom. Except for the other reporters and the lawyers, there was no one in the courtroom. Jackson shuffled toward a seat behind the table at which Montrose, Antonia and Manuelito talked quietly. He took the notebook from his pocket and waited in the quiet courtroom.

Just before the final deadline last night, Jackson had called the newsroom to dictate a fresh lead to the story since Manuelito was now back in custody and headed for the Santa Fe County juvenile detention center and today's arraignment. His night editor had been curt but polite, and said she was not accustomed to being hung up on. Jackson had mumbled an apology.

In the morning he had driven back to Santa Fe with Ariel on his mind and thinking how it could be with her. He thought of her tawny hair, her young body and her smooth, fair skin and how it felt against his. No. Stop it, he thought. You're just thinking of yourself. It had been long, though, very long since he had woken up in the morning beside a woman, someone to caress and to kiss and with whom to make slow, sleepy love.

"All rise," the clerk's voice intoned. "The First Judicial Court of the State of New Mexico is now in session. The honorable Judge Alfonso Ortega presiding." The crowd stood as a hunched, curly-haired judge entered, took his seat, and banged the gavel. He surveyed the courtroom with narrow eyes behind rimless glasses.

"Is everyone here?" Judge Ortega glanced at Montrose and the prosecutor, an athletic-looking man with thinning, hair, who wore pleated khaki pants and an oxford cloth, button-down blue shirt with a red paisley tie under a gray herring bone sport coat. Ortega cleared his throat. "I want to register the court's dismay of the procedural moves that have been made so far. The executive branch of government, which possesses most of the police powers of this country, does not make agreements that bind the judicial branch." Pausing for emphasis, he stared at both attorneys. "However, in this case, and particularly in the interest of public peace and harmony, I am willing to go along with this. So, this is an arraignment at which we will presumably set a preliminary hearing date."

Jackson jotted a few notes, but paused as Ortega droned on about the procedures and glanced around room again asking, "Is the defendant here?"

Montrose stood. "Your honor. I am Richard Montrose representing Manuelito Aguilar. Seated to my right here is his mother, Antonia Aguilar. Manuelito pleads not guilty," he said.

The judge set the preliminary hearing for following Monday, only five days away.

Montrose objected, saying that he could not prepare a reasonable defense in so short time and the court had to allow him more time to review the evidence. "Also, we don't have an autopsy report," Montrose said. "We have no reports on the cause of death. The corpse of El Viejo has to be exhumed and examined if the body is not too badly decomposed. The report must be made available."

Judge Ortega nodded. "Let's get an autopsy report and return to this courtroom and then we'll have a hearing with some facts in hand."

The prosecutor frowned and shook his head.

Montrose smiled.

Turning his attention to Manuelito and Antonia, Judge Ortega explained that the crime of which Manuelito had been accused was very serious, a capital offense. Of course, an accusation did not imply guilt. Considering that Manuelito never been in trouble before, he would be released into the custody of his mother and his attorney, the court trusting that they would be responsible and insure that he appear at the preliminary hearing. Montrose and Antonia nodded. "The court is adjourned," Ortega said, banging the gavel.

Jackson reached across the railing that separated the public from the rest of the court and tapped Montrose on the shoulder. "What do you think?"

Montrose smiled. "Ortega wants to put this off as long as possible. The only evidence they have is Manuelito's fingerprints on the gun. But that's nothing. The question is what kind of bullet killed the old man. The autopsy should tell us." He hustled Antonia and Manuelito across the courtroom and disappeared through the doorway to the judge's chambers.

§

The television and newspaper cameramen slumped outside, lifting baseball hats to wipe sweat from their foreheads. Reporter notebooks were used like sun shades. Sheriff's deputies and state policemen shifted from foot to foot, waiting, occasionally turning their heads to speak quietly into microphones hooked to their epaulets. A breeze stirred. Jackson looked to where Brock fanned herself with a notebook, and adjusted her sunglasses. Montrose, Antonia, and Manuelito squinted as they suddenly came out through the courthouse doors and walked quickly down the courthouse steps.

"Any comments?" Brock barked.

"No!" Montrose replied.

"Do you think the prosecutor has a case?"

Montrose shook his head. "A grandchild does not shoot a grandfather he loves in cold blood. I don't mind telling you that Manuelito found the old man dead, then reported the crime. He's a brave young man."

"What about the fingerprints?" Brock asked.

Montrose waved his hand. "That's easily explained. Look, this will all come out in the hearing. We have to leave." He pushed past the cameras.

"Do you think your son did it?" one of the television reporters asked Antonia. She stopped abruptly.

"That's a rude question," she said, scowling. "Of course not." Her words hung in the air. She slipped an arm gently around Manuelito's shoulder and they moved carefully through the crowd.

※23※

Tierra Amarilla

The backhoe bucket dropped with a noisy *thunk.* Thick steel teeth bit into the dirt. The operator worked the yellow levers. The dirt was scooped, lifted, and dumped to the side with a clank and a jerk. Dust drifted in the air. Jackson watched mutely, arms crossed as the teeth bit into the dirt again and the bucket scooped and dumped once more.

"I can't watch this," Antonia said, turning to walk back to the weaving store.

It had been difficult to position the backhoe so not to mar the other churchyard graves covered with dried weeds and grass. Faded plastic flowers in toppled glass vases adorned simple gravestones, some tilted as if weary of decades of standing erect. A portion of the graveyard fencing had been folded back against itself.

The door to the church opened and a black-robed priest with a receding hairline and bushy mustache stepped into the sun, squinting. He shook his head and crossed himself, then with deliberation, descended the short steps. His body bent slightly forward, hands clasp behind him, he stood beside Jackson who sat on a rounded, upright gravestone. Over the revving of the backhoe's engine, the priest moved toward Jackson and said with disgust, "The dead should not be disturbed."

Jackson adjusted his sunglasses. "Yeah. They're really grumpy when they're woken up." The priest nodded uncertainly, then scowled.

"I will pray for the souls of the dearly departed as well as the souls of those still among us," the priest said sanctimoniously, then turned to make his way back to the church.

Yeah, pray for me, Jackson thought. I need it.

A loud clunk came from the grave. The backhoe operator grimaced and looked at Montrose. The engine idled and the operator jumped off. Shovel in hand, he stepped down into the grave and carefully scraped dirt from the casket. The wood casket was cracked, splintered. "It's a lot shallower than they said," the operator complained. He began to use his spade to remove the dirt. Once finished, he climbed back out and brushed his hands on his jeans.

With the casket fully exposed, the operator struggled to slip straps under it. Jackson and the others helped to tug and heave and he was surprised that the casket was surprisingly light. But as it was brought it up and into the sunlight, the awful stench of a decomposing body was in the air. Brushing off the dirt, they hoisted it onto the shoved dirt then carried it to the medical investigator's mini-van. Jackson gagged at the smell.

"I hope you're driving with the windows open," Jackson said to the investigator, who ignored him.

"It'll be a week, give or take," the investigator said to Montrose. "We're really backed up."

"There's a lot riding on this," Montrose said.

"There always is," the investigator said. The van lurched forward and drove away.

Jackson turned back to the grave. The backhoe operator had thrown a sheet of plywood over the gaping hole and was backing his machine out of the graveyard.

§

The grass was flattened, wilting in the sun and a warm wind pushed him gently. Only tire tracks remained where Jackson and the state police had gathered outside the protest camp less than forty-eight hours earlier. Cicadas buzzed. No guard was obvious. And, no police. Nothing. The scene felt haunted, lifeless. He scanned the camp, but detected no movement. He parked at the side of the road, climbed out, crossed the cattle guard, and made his way up the road to the campfire. He crouched and held out his hands. The fire was only ash, but it was still warm. He poked at the embers with a stick. Smoke and ash swirled. Overhead the Mexican flag fluttered weakly. Then El Cuchillo, ski mask on, came out of the trailer and limped over to Jackson. "What are you doing here?"

Jackson was quiet. "Thought I'd see how you're doing."

El Cuchillo yawned, stretched, and let out a big, moaning sigh.

"But my timing's not so good," Jackson said. "Looks like everyone's gone."

"They'll be back," El Cuchillo said. He walked over to a canvass covering with several aluminum chairs folded under it. He handed one to Jackson. "Sit. Want some coffee?"

"Sure."

El Cuchillo leaned forward and put his hand on the blackened coffee pot. "Hmm. Not too warm." He grabbed a stick and stirred the coals. He stood with a groan, grabbed three small logs and shoved them under the grate. "It'll be a minute." El Cuchillo settled into his chair. Waving a finger, he said, "Get a couple cups."

Jackson took two Styrofoam cups from a bag. "I want to spend some time here, live at the camp. Write some stories about the people here."

The logs began to smolder, then the smoke became flame. El Cuchillo had bloodshot eyes. "You want to write about the camp?"

Jackson nodded, waited. "My editors think it's a great idea."

El Cuchillo looked off across the empty fields to the mountains. "I don't know. I'll have to clear it with the *consejo* before we do anything like that."

Aw hell, Jackson thought. Publicity was the only thing keeping this protest from being squashed by the police and he knew it. But El Cuchillo was going to play it cool, like a woman who knows she's being pursued. It's the chase, not the capture, that makes it interesting. Sure, Jackson thought. I can wait for a *consejo* decision.

"The first thing you have to realize is that this is a people's movement," El Cuchillo said. "We're not just a bunch of crazies. The reason no one's here now is simple. They have families. They have business to take care of. They are part of this camp, this protest, because they believe in it."

"The police wasted no time to make themselves scarce."

El Cuchillo shook his head. "The police don't really care about us. They just wanted to make a point, put on a show of force."

The blue enamel coffee pot ticked. El Cuchillo picked it up splashed coffee into the cups. Jackson settled back. He knew that if the police truly wanted to end this, they would walk in and take El Cuchillo. "You're alone?"

El Cuchillo nodded.

Jackson scanned the camp. The silence was discomforting.

"They are so stupid," El Cuchillo said disdainfully. "They could walk in now and arrest me. But they don't really want me."

※24※

Tierra Amarilla

Jackson unrolled his sleeping bag on the foam pad and shook it to get some loft in the stuffing material. It had been packed too long. His foot banged against a wooden case. He turned and stooped to pull it out of the way. He lifted the lid. The grenade launcher was there along with the grenades. He had used one once, but it had been many years ago, during his basic weapons training in the army. He had never been good at it, but some guys could drop a grenade in a foxhole or through the window of a building. Jackson had trained to fire most other weapons as well, from the shoulder-held, anti-tank weapons to the sixty-caliber machine guns. The thought of carrying the machine gun through the jungles of Vietnam had appalled him. He preferred the M-16s, the light rifles with the black plastic stocks and barrel grips. Made by Mattel, they're swell, is what the soldiers had said about them. The shots popped and the guns had very little kick, which suited him just fine.

He hoisted the grenade launcher and inspected it. It had been cleaned and smelled of oil. This was a drastic act, he thought, a desperate and dangerous measure for these protestors. Old and historic social wounds were being reopened by this protest, wounds that had never healed.

"You like that?"

Jackson turned to the sound.

Trini's frame was silhouetted in the entrance to the bunker. "It was my favorite. Vietnam. Took out lots of them with it." He waited for Jackson to respond, then said, "You know how to use it?"

"Sort of," Jackson said.

Trini took it, pushed the top lever to one side. It fell open. He stooped, picked up a grenade, slipped it into the fat tubular barrel and snapped it shut. "Aim and shoot. That's it." He snapped it open again. The grenade fell out into his hand. He handed the grenade and launcher to Jackson who repeated his movements. Trini smiled. "You got it."

"I hope this never gets used," Jackson said.

Trini smiled, shrugged. "You never know." He pushed his cowboy hat back on his head. "This is usually my bunker, but El Cuchillo says it's yours for as long as you're here." He patted the sleeping bag. "This foam pad under here is pretty comfortable, once you get used to it."

"Seems pretty good." Jackson carefully replaced the grenade and launcher in the wooden box and pushed it back under the planks.

"There's food out there, if you're hungry."

"Thanks."

Smoke drifted through the camp. The distant Brazos cliffs in the mountains were red-orange in the fading light. The clank of a bell caught his attention. A large shaggy ram with gnarled and curving horns was tied to a tree. The ram pulled back against the rope that tethered it. Head erect, the ram watched with steely eyes as Jackson passed. The bell clanked again as the ram jerked against the rope.

"That old boy's not too happy," Trini said.

Antonia looked up from the paper plate on her lap. "So you're here to get a scoop?"

"I guess." Jackson said.

"Well, you can start by getting a scoop of food." She glanced at Trini and chuckled. "Help yourself," motioning with her fork. "Mutton. Specialty of the house."

"Thanks, I'll get some in a minute." Jackson went to his truck, opened the back of the camper shell, and let down the tail gate. He found his hiking boots. Looping the leather laces around the metal hooks, he tied them tight. He closed the back of the truck and gave passing thought to locking up his briefcase and computer. No need. No one around here would take it.

Back at the camp, a cast iron pot bubbled on the grate and beside it a flat pan with chunks of meat simmered. He ladled beans from the pot, drained off the excess liquid, and dumped them onto his plate, inhaling the aroma. He piled on chunks of roasted mutton.

"Salt and pepper's there," Antonia said. Jackson nodded and took some.

He was hungry, hungrier than he had thought. Sitting on a fat block of wood near the fire, he took a bite.

Manuelito rode through the camp on a small mountain bike with knobby tires. He slid to a stop near his mother.

"I told you no racing through the camp," Antonia said, her voice sharp, her eyes soft.

"I wasn't, mom," he said, looking away. He stood on his pedals and slowly headed down the road to the gate, passing between the loops of barbed wire.

"I worry about him," Antonia said. "They had no right," she said bitterly. Her eyes were glassy, dark. She cleared her throat, as if it had gotten thick. "They walked right into the school, did you know that? There were three squad cars. Told the principal to go get him out of class. Wanted to talk to him, they said. Then they arrested him." She stared at Jackson. "What pigs they are that they would do that. The principal, my cousin, called me right away. By the time we got to Espanola, they were already there, at the jailhouse. They were going to take him to the Santa Fe County Juvenile Detention Center, but we talked them out of it." Poking at the last of her food, she tossed the paper plate in the fire. The edges blackened and curled, the grease crackled. She brushed her hands on her jeans. "First El Viejo, now this. What next?" Her dark eyes flashed. "Sometimes I forget we are just simple people trying to make our way in the world." She rose, found a cup, filled it with coffee, then returned to her chair. She blew across it before sipping. "When I was a child, life was simple. We raised our sheep. We lived off of them. We always had whatever we needed. Then something changed." She stared solemnly into the fire. "It became harder and harder to raise the sheep. The wool market disappeared. The pastures were gone. Everything is different now."

Jackson held his cup under the spigot of a blue five-gallon water cooler, filled it and drank with deep, long gulps. He refilled it and drank again.

"Isn't it just the times?" he said. "More people, but no more land?"

She shrugged. "No. No. It's more than that. We're being forced out, squeezed out."

"No one can force people to sell their land."

"You think not?" she asked incredulously. "They can make people want to just give up. That's what they do. They get tired of having to fight for the right to graze their sheep, fight for the rights they've had for many generations. It's a lot of hard work for very little money. They sell out. They move to Albuquerque. Work for Intel. Can you believe it? Intel. They herd computer chips now instead of sheep." She smiled weakly and sipped.

"The way of the world, isn't it?"

Her eyes flared, angry again. "Is it the way of the world when everything is taken from you, piece by piece?" She almost came out of her chair, but paused and sat back. "First the hunting is cut off." She slapped her hands. "Then the grazing is cut off." She slapped her hands again. "Then the houses are sold, one by one. Some people don't even sell. They just move away. They board up the houses and go away." She fell silent and gazed into the flames. "It's so sad. So sad." She cleared her throat. "You know El Valle? The Village?"

Jackson nodded.

"Every building used to be occupied. There were stores, a gas station. The building we're in now used to be a big general store. Stuff was stacked on the shelves all the way to the ceiling: bolts of cloth, clothes, radios, tools, guns, fishing poles and big jars of candy on the counter. I thought that store was the most amazing place in the world." She sighed. "You know what I miss the most? It's the feeling. We used to know everyone, all the secrets. This was a real place. If someone was in trouble, they got help. Strangers came, strangers went. But we stayed. It was all real good." Her voice drifted off. She lifted her eyes to him. "That's what we are fighting for. We want our village back."

Wind rustled through the trees, pushing the flames.

"It's time to walk the walk," Sixto said, stepping suddenly into the firelight. He handed a leather holster to Antonia. She buckled it around her waist. "Guard duty," Sixto said to Jackson. "Everyone takes a shift. We walk the perimeter."

Jackson nodded.

"Me and Antonia will take nine to midnight," Sixto said. "You want midnight to three, or three to six? El Cuchillo likes the three to six. He's asleep now."

"It doesn't matter," Jackson said.

"We need someone at midnight," he said. "You can go with

Tomas."

"Okay."

"Better get some sleep now. I'll wake you."

Jackson wandered outside the glow of the campfire to his truck where he fished his flashlight from the glove compartment. Tapping it on the palm of his hand, the light brightened, then slowly faded. "Damn," he said. The batteries dead, he put the flashlight back into the compartment.

Back at the camp, he skirted the campfire and stepped down into the dark bunker. He sat on the edge of his sleeping bag. He admired Antonia for her deep commitment to community, but she was trying to stop the tide. Her talk had left him feeling hollow. Now he wondered if it had been such a good idea for him to be there. He had pitched it hard to his editor and he had liked it. But now, Jackson felt like he was part of the problem that Antonia was fighting. He was making their situation worse, not better. Now the entire world would peer into their lives, via the news media. But, he told himself, if he wasn't there, then someone else would be, some reporter who didn't really give a damn.

In fact, there was nothing Antonia or El Cuchillo or anyone else could do. Sooner or later the tide would come swirling in around and overwhelm everything. He shook his head, kicked off his boots and stretched out on the sleeping bag. Who had killed El Viejo? It was now an afterthought, a footnote. The death had launched the protest, but now the protest had its own set of wheels, its own momentum. He pressed the night light on his watch: 9:10. A few hours of sleep before his guard shift, a few after. It would be all right. He heard footsteps nearby. They paused, then went on. It must be Sixto and Antonia. He lay still.

The moon emerged again from behind dark clouds, lighting the land. Jackson sat up and looked out. It was ghostly. What if the police came in the middle of the night? Don't think about it. He fell back onto the bag, slipping his arm behind his head. He had told Ariel he would probably spend a few days at the camp. She said it was all right. Be careful, she said, and hugged him; then, looking into eyes, she kissed him. He was beginning to miss her. It would be a long night. He shouldn't have had the coffee. He didn't need to be awake now. Jackson closed his eyes. Sometimes he heard footsteps, but he couldn't be sure. He thought of Luna, and then of Margo and Fredrickson and the big house and the dogs, and of his own casita. Of the computer in his truck, the stories he had to write, stories about the camp. A disappearing way of life. People flocking to the West, a new migration, fleeing the big cities, fleeing the crime, the random and senseless crime. Abandoning the cities and the pollution, the madness. Now they were bringing it with them.

※25※

Tierra Amarilla

A hand shook Jackson's arm. He blinked gritty, resisting eyes. Yellow light filled the bunker. Sixto's dark eyes stared down at him. His flashlight pointed to the corrugated metal of the bunker roof.

"Yeah. I'm awake," Jackson said, sitting up and rubbing his eyes. He focused on his watch. 12:15. "God. I slept." He clicked on his own flashlight as Sixto left the bunker. Jackson felt like he had not slept at all. He stretched his aching muscles. He wanted to lie back down. Move, he told himself, move. He pulled on his hiking boots and fumbled with his laces. This is what I wanted. To live at the camp, to experience it all. For a story, a stinking story. He climbed out of the bunker and walked through the trees toward the campfire. He entered the fire light and poured himself a cup of scalding hot coffee. It burned the tip of his tongue.

"Here." Sixto handed him a folded black leather gun belt and with the holstered gun.

Jackson buckled it around his waist and it hung heavy on his hips. Jesus, he thought, what am I getting myself into? What if I really have to use this thing? He unsnapped the cover and lifted the forty-five caliber automatic pistol out of the holster, pointing the barrel skyward. Shoot a cop? Hardly. He'd never do it. But this was part of the deal, El Cuchillo said. If he was to live at the camp, he had to do what everyone did, including walk the perimeter on guard duty. You agreed, Jackson thought. You knew El Cuchillo was testing you, challenging you to show your true sympathies. But what are they? Even you don't know, he thought. You spent your whole life sitting on the sidelines, watching and writing, but never participating. El Cuchillo was now giving you a chance to change that. An exclusive chance to get inside it all.

"Is this loaded?"

Sixto nodded gravely.

"The weapon of last resort."

"Best be armed. Let's take a walk. Bring your coffee."

Jackson slipped the gun back into the holster and snapped the cover. They walked to the skinny strand of rolled barbed wire. In the distance, an occasional house light glowed in the sea of moonlight and shadows. Beyond that, the granite Brazos cliffs were ghostly pale.

"Pssst." Sixto motioned for him to hurry. "If you're late, it means something happened. People get nervous." They circled the camp, passing the bunkers, pausing to listen and scan the fields. When they returned, El Cuchillo, unmasked, sat slouched in a folding chair at the fire. He had a round face, and large, sad eyes. Laced fingers rested on his stomach. "*Buenas noches,*" El Cuchillo said. He looked tired. El Cuchillo slowly lifted his eyes to Jackson, then dropped his gaze to the flames.

"I thought you'd be sleeping," Jackson said, refilling his coffee.

"All I need is three, maybe four hours of sleep a night," El Cuchillo said, as if sleep was a nuisance. He rubbed his face with his hands, then reached for his coffee. "I nap in the afternoon sometimes."

Sixto's face stretched into a big yawn. "I like my six hours. I'm turning in." He groaned and mumbled some Spanish.

"*Donde esta Tomas?*" El Cuchillo asked.

Sixto shrugged and disappeared into the shadows. Moments later a young man stumbled into the light, eyes cloudy with sleep. His pant legs were half tucked into beat up cowboy boots, his shirt unbuttoned and dangling.

El Cuchillo spoke to him sharply as Tomas ran his hand through his disheveled hair and replaced his cap before shuffling to the coffee pot. "*Andale*, it's your shift," El Cuchillo said. "Where's your gun?"

"*La troka*," Tomas said, referring to his truck. He splashed coffee into a white cup, spilling it on his hand. "Aiiee," he said, dropping the cup to the ground. He looked sheepishly at El Cuchillo, who waved for him to go. Tomas slouched to the edge of the firelight and opened the door of a faded red pickup. He lifted a bolt-action rifle from the rear window rack and slipped the leather sling over his shoulder. The door creaked as he slammed it shut, then vanished into the darkness.

El Cuchillo shook his head and sighed. "He's a good man, but you gotta stay on top of him."

Jackson nodded and sat on a block of pine. He leaned forward and stared into the crackling, hissing fire. It was like they were the only two people in the world. Jackson held out his hands to the warmth. "What made you do this?"

El Cuchillo contemplated him. "Is this an interview?"

Jackson returned El Cuchillo's gaze. He was not going to make it easy. "What do you do when you're not fighting the government?"

El Cuchillo stood slowly, rubbed his arms protruding from his down vest, then picked up a couple of pieces of wood and tossed them on the fire. Sparks rose.

"I drive a school bus." He glanced at Jackson quickly then at the fire.

A school bus driver? Jackson thought. It seemed incongruous. El Cuchillo pointed off into the darkness. "I got a house, some land, over there, a few miles from El Valle. I got sheep, part of the community flock. I helped Antonia get the wool co-op going."

"You from here?"

He shook his head and sat down. "I was born here. My grandparents live in Monte Vista. They raised me up in Colorado." He flexed his hand and considered it, as if he had never seen it before. "I was gonna be a priest. Went to college for a while. Adams State in Alamosa."

"Did you finish?"

He shook his head. "Dropped out. Then the draft board came after me. They wanted more Mexicans in the army, so I went underground in sixty-eight."

Jackson smiled. "People don't remember how crazy it was back then."

El Cuchillo nodded.

"So, how'd you end up back here?"

"After a couple years they caught up with me in Los Angeles. They arrested me, accused me of helping to blow up the Bank of America. Wanted me to rat on some people, but I wouldn't." He sipped his coffee. "They put me in prison for a few months. They thought

I'd crack, but I didn't." He leaned back, stretched his arms above his head. The memories came back. "They said I was blocking a federal investigation...something like that. It really doesn't matter. They can trump up charges and toss you in jail whenever they want."

"I vaguely remember that Bank of America thing. You were involved?"

The flames glowed orange on El Cuchillo's face. "They said dynamite came from the construction of the dam over there on the Rio Chama. But they could never prove it."

Jackson looked into the fire, then directly at him. "Did you do it?"

El Cuchillo smiled, pondering an answer. He had revealed something and Jackson wanted more. He waited a long time before he spoke again. "If I did, do you think I'd admit it?"

"Reporters know lots of things that never get printed."

El Cuchillo's eyes hardened. "Bullshit. Reporters print nothing but lies."

Jackson felt stung. He swallowed. "That's not true. We...I write the truth as best I can. Sometimes it's hard to find, especially when people won't talk to you."

"What do you know of the truth?"

Jackson swallowed again. "I know what I see. I know what people tell me."

"That's not an answer," El Cuchillo said. "The media prints lies, nothing but lies."

Jackson shook his head. He looked intently at El Cuchillo. "Sometimes truth is in the eye of the beholder."

El Cuchillo just stared back.

Damn, Jackson thought. Here I sit with a goddam gun on my hip that could get me killed and this guy is barking at me. "So why did you let me here?"

"Antonia. She likes you. She thinks it will help our cause."

"And you don't?"

El Cuchillo flared. "We don't need your goddam sympathy," he growled. "We need our land back. The only way that's going to happen is by force." He pounded his fist into his hand with a loud smack. Jackson flinched. The fire danced in El Cuchillo's eyes. "You guys are going to write whatever you're going to write. It just doesn't matter and I don't give a damn about you or any of the rest of them."

The fire crackled. El Cuchillo rose and went to a pile of wood, grabbed a couple more small pieces and jammed them under the grate, raising a swirl of glowing red sparks.

Jackson swallowed hard. "You think you can win?"

El Cuchillo thought for a moment. "You think we can't?"

Against people like Chief Woodward and Governor Carrow? Jackson thought. Against the goddam national guard? This was the kind of thing those guys live for. Law and order to the max. And, the public loved it. El Cuchillo had given them an excuse. And they would kill him easily. Jackson felt sorry for him. Surely he understood.

El Cuchillo lifted his eyes from the fire and looked at Jackson.

Yes, Jackson thought. He knows.

"Why the name?"

"The knife? *El Cuchillo?*" He pronounced it with a flourish and a wave of his hand, looking into the night. "It's a deadly weapon. *Que no*?"

Jackson nodded. Or soon a dead weapon, he thought. Coming into the fire light, Tomas unslung his rifle and rested it against the table. He poured himself another coffee.

"You awake now?" El Cuchillo asked.

Tomas nodded slightly.

"What about Tomas here?" Jackson asked. "What motivates him?"

El Cuchillo spoke Spanish to him and nodded toward Jackson.

"*La tierra*," Tomas said with quiet conviction. The land.

"*Nada mas*?" Jackson asked.

"*Los churros*," he said.

"The sheep?"

El Cuchillo nodded.

"Simple enough."

"People here understand what's at stake."

"What about the police?" Jackson asked. "What if they storm this place?"

El Cuchillo calmly looked at Tomas and spoke in Spanish. Tomas replied. El Cuchillo translated. "He says he is not afraid to die and is not afraid of the police." Then he added, "*viva la revolucion.*"

※26※

Tierra Amarilla

Daylight flooded the bunker. A truck started, the engine revving. It clunked into gear and drove away. Another truck started, the sound fading as it too drove away. Manuelito's voice sounded faintly, then a few moments later the whir of a bicycle passing by the bunker. "No, he's not awake yet," Manuelito yelled.

Comfortable and warm in his sleeping bag, Jackson looked at his watch: 7:15. The top of this section of the bunker was six-inch diameter logs covered with plywood and dirt. Jackson tugged on his jeans, tied his boots, and climbed out and into the morning. Antonia sat in a folding chair near the smoldering campfire. Manuelito energetically rode his bicycle around the camp. The place again felt abandoned, and Jackson wondered why he was there. Had he been enticed by a story that existed only in the mind of El Cuchillo, Antonia, and maybe a few others?

"*Buenas dias*, *Senor*," Antonia said with mock formality.

Jackson felt embarrassed as if he had over slept.

"*Huevos*? They're fresh."

"Sure. That'd be nice," Jackson said.

"I'll fix 'em for you," Antonia said. With practiced movements, she dolloped lard into a small cast-iron skillet and waited while it warmed and became clear, then cracked two large brown eggs into it that sizzled and bubbled at the edges. She stirred them with a fork, then moved the skillet to the side of the fire beside the pan of cooked mutton. She forked a few chunks of meat into the pan and mixed them with the eggs, then scrapped the contents onto a paper plate that she handed to Jackson. He nodded a thank you and sat on the pine block and ate hungrily. Antonia wiped her hands with a paper towel and tossed it into the fire, watching it flame quickly. "El Cuchillo told me you found out about some money at the Legislature." She looked at him curiously.

Jackson ate a forkful of eggs. "At the last minute, the Legislature appropriated some money for the Johnson Wildlife Area. But it's not clear what that money means. It could be for anything. Habitat improvement, game wardens, security. Who knows?"

She became dark and stern. "See? It's just as I thought. Governor Carrow tells me and the *consejo* that he's doing everything he can to help us. But he's not. He's giving money to those wildlife people so they can fight us."

"You're up against a lot of money and power," Jackson said, trying to sympathize.

"*Pendejos*—assholes."

§

After a long, hot shower late that morning at Ariel's room at the hot springs, and a change of clothes, Jackson called Stacy at the *Herald*. "It's pretty tame," Jackson said apologetically. "The cops are gone. Protesters at the site come and go as they please."

"Hmmm. Stick with it. Get below the surface," Stacy said. "Lots of color. I want it for a big Sunday spread across two pages."

"Well, I hope something happens to give this story some legs. Right now, there's not much," Jackson said.

"We need photos. Got your camera?"

"Of course. I'll send you some images later today."

"Good."

Jackson hung up and made a quick but fruitless search of the spa for Ariel. He had to get back to the camp. Photos with the story helped it come alive and gave it weight. As he drove back toward El Valle, headlines came to him. "Life at the camp remains calm despite the tensions of the past week." That won't do, he thought.

Jackson turned off the highway, just past the billboard, and dipped down the sharply curving road to El Valle village. Ariel's black Saab was parked by the side of the road. He hit the brakes, pulled over and parked. Over his shoulder he saw a dirt path that lead to a shrine in the cliffs. He wondered how he could have missed that. He'd come by this place a dozen times.

Ariel knelt, her posture mimicking a bright white statue in the rocks she faced above, a praying Mother Mary. Above that was a much larger statue of Jesus, hands touched in prayer. Glassed candles flickered beside bright plastic flowers scattered among the rocks. It was a quiet spot, hidden, shrouded by trees, sacred, secret, serene, protected by a stone arch and topped by a concrete cross. Jackson hesitated at a white handrail. He approached apprehensively. Ariel's lips quivered in repetitive prayer, her eyes closed. Jackson put a hand gently on her shoulder. She turned her head reflexively, not stopping, then bowed her head again. Jackson retreated, paused at the handrail, then walked to his truck.

He thought about leaving, but waited. Ariel stood slowly after several more minutes, using her hands to push herself up. She bent stiffly to brush dirt from her knees. She struck a match and rekindled several candles. She backed away, paused, and bowed. She sluggishly made her way to her car, opened the door, then looked at Jackson. "What are you doing here?"

"I should ask you that question."

"I was praying," she said dully, speaking across the roof of the Saab.

"Are you okay?"

"Of course." She cocked her head, as if the question was strange.

"How come you're here?"

"Haven't you heard of prayer?" she said, as if no explanation was needed.

"I didn't know you were so devout."

She looked away, out across the roofs of the village, to the green patchwork fields. The faded pink church stood brightly in the morning sun, its white cross shining in the blue sky. "I went to see the *curandera*. She lives here. She gave me some herbs. We drank some tea. She's good. I feel much better." She spoke slowly, looking at him with distant eyes. "She told me to pray, that it would help the medicine work."

Perhaps, Jackson thought. He took her in his arms. She put her head against his chest. "I'm worried about you, Ariel," he said. He kissed her head, inhaled deeply, and absorbed the warmth of her body.

"I know," she murmured.

※27※

Tierra Amarilla

"Shoot it!" Antonia said.

The ram jerked against the rope and stood still, staring with gray-yellow eyes.

Trini raised the rifle, his right hand gripping the trigger, his left on the front grip. The ram stepped sideways and faced Trini. He lowered the rifle. "Luis, get its back legs," he shouted and waved the rifle. Luis adjusted his baseball cap, loosened a coil of rope and swung it handily over his head. He threw it to the ground, lassoed the ram's hind legs and jerked, lifting them off the ground. The ram was balanced on its two front legs.

"All right, Luis," Antonia shouted, clapping her hands.

Luis grinned broadly and held the rope tight. Hind legs stretched, the ram struggled. It looked pathetic, neck straining, standing on its two front legs. Trini lifted his rifle. A sharp crack rang out. The ram was knocked sideways to the ground. Luis relaxed the rope, and the rear legs of the ram jerked wildly, its front legs pumping. Jackson's stomach tightened.

"He missed the heart," Antonia said with troubled eyes. "If he hits the heart, it dies right away. There is no pain." The ram kicked and tried to bleat, but emitted only choking sounds. Blood ran from its mouth, its tongue protruded. "Poor thing. You hit the lungs," she yelled.

Trini ran over to the ram, poked the barrel against its head, and pulled the trigger. The shot was muffled. The ram shuddered and went stiff.

"Okay," Antonia said, kneeling beside it. "That's better. The knife," she ordered, and held out her hand. Trini unsheathed his hunting knife and handed it to her, handle first. Antonia jerked the ram's head back, felt its throat, then cut it. She slipped a metal bowl under the wide slash to catch the blood. "If it's done soon enough, the blood comes out. The meat is cleaner," she said to Jackson. "Luis, move the legs uphill." Luis swung the rear of the ram up the slight slope. "*Bueno.*" Dark blood dribbled from the slit throat into the bowl. Antonia worked the neck with a hand, squeezing it. Jackson watched her curiously. She smiled, said something in Spanish to Luis and Trini and they laughed.

"It's for pudding. Blood pudding. I've got to get the stuff out of it that makes it hard. Otherwise it's no good."

"Coagulants."

She nodded, her hand coated with blood. Occasionally she threw a clot to the ground. "Damn," she said. "There's hardly enough." She looked at Luis. "We'd better string him up, let it drain."

Luis tossed the rope over a thick pine tree branch overhead, pulling hard. Trini helped. The hind legs of the ram were dragged along the ground and then ascended until its front legs cleared the ground. Antonia tilted the ram's head back, blood oozing from the gash, trickling off the wool and into the bowl. "When we butcher an animal, we use all of it."

Jackson nodded. It was gruesome work, he thought, but it had to be done.

"Hold this. My hands are tired."

Jackson grabbed the thick, rippled ram horns, lifting the head up and back. It was heavy, limp and lifeless.

"Whose ram was this?"

Luis smiled. "He was a good ram, but he was too old. He was knocking down the fences, getting into trouble. We got others, younger ones that are no trouble."

"Luis donated this to the cause," Antonia said. Luis smiled and watched Antonia as she continued to massage the neck. Green, iridescent flies buzzed above her hand, landing at the edges of the bowl. She sat back, sighed and brushed her forehead with the back of her hand. "That's it," she said, swirling the contents, looking at it with dissatisfaction. "Hardly worth the trouble."

Jackson took pictures as Trini skinned the animal, slicing straight down the abdomen to the throat, exposing the guts. He pulled at the hide, slipping the knife delicately between it and the flesh, slicing the white membrane. Luis muttered a few words in Spanish to Trini and they laughed.

"He said this old bastard is going to be tough to eat, just like he was when he was alive," Trini said.

"We'll just have to cook the hell out of it," Luis said with a laugh.

"What'd you call him?"

Luis shook his head. "The old ram. We never give a name to something we might have to eat."

They stripped the hide completely. The smell of skinned flesh filled the air.

Luis held the hide high. "You want it?"

Jackson was dumbfounded. "I don't know."

Luis laughed. "A sheepskin. You can be a graduate. *La universidad de la vida.*" Jackson smiled weakly.

§

A thick leg of the sheep roasted on the grate, dripping grease that occasionally flared from the glowing coals. The sheep's carcass had been portioned and packed in ice under tarps in two large coolers under the kitchen table. A dozen people milled around the camp as the setting sun cast long shadows. The sky was clear; the wind had dropped. Wood was stacked near the fire where a large black caldron bubbled and the scent of cooking *posole* drifted in the air. An elderly woman, gray hair tied with a handkerchief, used gnarled fingers to turn a dozen large green chiles on the grate. She looked kindly at Jackson with deeply set eyes. He clicked a frame off in his camera. She looked up shyly from her etched face. She waved her hand as if he was a bothersome fly. She turned the roasted green and blistered chile pods. Setting one on a paper plate, the old woman deftly removed the skin and sliced the pepper with a short knife. She popped a piece into her mouth, glancing mischievously at Jackson. She scraped the rest into the pot of *posole*. She reached for another, peeled it and offered a chunk to Jackson. He put it in his mouth. It burned. The old woman watched expectantly. He exhaled and waved his hand in front of his mouth as if to cool it, then chewed quickly. She laughed with a toothless smile. He went to the water cooler and drew a cup.

"No, no," the old woman said, waving the knife. "*Miel*—honey."

Jackson knew she was right. Cold water did nothing to cool the hot chile taste, but sweetness eased the burn.

He returned his camera to his truck, and from there surveyed the camp, watching the slow pace, the smoke rising into the clear sky as the sun finally dropped below the distant hills. The Brazos rock faced to the west, gray and solid in the afternoon sun, now glowed orange. Cars on the nearby highway glinted fitfully. He took a deep breath and felt a bulge in his jacket pocket. He pulled out the clear plastic bag that Ariel had given to him. Tea, she said, a small gift for his camping adventure. He fished through the back of his truck and found a small, black coffee pot among his gear.

He returned to the camp, filled it with water and put it on the fire. The old woman cut the final chile. She looked at his baggie curiously. He handed it to her. She smelled it. "*Yerba buena*," she said, nodding. He emptied some of it into the pot of water, then stood back and waited. The water heated quickly and he poured two cups, handing her one. She sipped the yellow-green tea with satisfaction.

"*Gracias*," she said.

Jackson inhaled the herbal scent and sipped.

Antonia jabbed the meat with a large fork. "This is ready," she announced. People gathered around, holding paper plates. She cut off thick slabs of meat and Jackson ladled out the puffy white *posole*. Later he sat quietly alone and ate. The meat was tough, as Luis had said, but it tasted good.

§

Quiet talk drifted in the air, the mood of the camp subdued. Remains of the roast had been removed from the fire and covered. The distant cliffs had mellowed to a soft purple, fading to gray-black. A bright moon rose over the mountains to the southeast, lighting the night.

The squeak of a musical instrument pierced the air. Luis slipped his arms through the straps and hoisted an accordion to his chest. He fiddled with the keys. The white box gleamed and sparkled in the firelight, emitting a mix of sounds. Luis sat on a stump, smiled and worked the accordion skillfully, playing a bouncy a Tex-Mex song. Feet tapped, hands clapped softly, faces brightened. Trini stepped toward the light, a fiddle tucked under his chin. He drew a bow across the strings, found the key, began to play with short, sawing motions. The two instruments sounded like an orchestra. The song finished on a high, stretched-out note that gently descended. Luis grinned at Trini and played a single note that Trini tried to match, then paused to tune the strings. They played again. Smiles flashed in firelight.

Antonia took Manuelito by the hands and they danced in a circle. Manuelito grinned and stumbled, looking embarrassed at his mother, not knowing what to do. She stepped easily sideways then forward and back as if in a square dance.

Sixto came out, a woman at his side, and the two danced spiritedly around the campfire, kicking up little clouds of dust. Others clapped, keeping the beat. As the song ended, Luis moved immediately into another, Trini following, sawing his bow lightly.

El Cuchillo, face bare, took Antonia and circled the campfire. A stout man, he moved gracefully with Antonia. Another couple joined in. The old woman of the chilies sat in a folding chair, her legs crossed at the ankles, a shawl over shoulders, clapping her hands and dancing with her dark eyes.

A loud crack broke the evening air. Sixto fell sideways, as if he had tripped, his partner still holding his hands. She toppled with him to the dusty ground at edge of the campfire.

Luis, open-mouthed, stopped playing, his last notes droning off key.

Sixto's chest oozed blood. He lay on the ground moaning.

"He's been shot!" El Cuchillo yelled, then turned to peer into the darkness. The camp was suddenly silent. The fire crackled. Trini grabbed El Cuchillo's arm.

"They could shoot again," Trini said. "Get everyone away from the fire."

"Cover everyone," El Cuchillo shouted, waving his arms and spinning, half crouched. He dropped to his knees beside Sixto, who coughed, blood at the edge of his mouth.

"We've got to get him to a hospital," Antonia said desperately, her eyes searching the faces of those nearby.

"Get him to the truck!" said Sixto's woman, her hand under his head. She pushed her hair back from her face.

"I'm coming with you!" Antonia said.

"We need to go right now!" the woman said in a panic.

Sixto cried out in pain as El Cuchillo, Luis and Antonia lifted him by the arms and legs.

"I have a mattress in the back of my truck," Jackson said, running to it in the darkness. He yanked the blankets off it carried it under an arm, the blankets under the other. Bernice dropped tailgate to one of the pickup trucks. Jackson tossed the foam mattress in and handed her the blankets. They hastily made a bed.

"He's hurt bad," El Cuchillo muttered as they lifted Sixto.

The moonlight reflected off Sixto's bloodied chest. Groaning, Sixto pulled himself onto the mattress and collapsed. Tears flowed down the woman's cheeks as she spread the blanket over him.

"I'll drive!" Antonia said.

"Hope he makes it," Jackson said awkwardly. He lifted the tailgate and closed the camper shell lid. The truck nosed down the moonlighted road. At the gate the head lights went on. Luis, El Cuchillo and Jackson stood and watched the truck disappear into the darkness. Several other trucks followed. The camp was suddenly quiet and empty.

"Where's Trini?" El Cuchillo asked sharply.

"He went after the sniper. Took his gun," Luis answered.

El Cuchillo turned again to the darkness. He took a spade, drove it into the ground with his foot, tossed dirt on the fire, killing the flames. The fire smoldered and smoke roiled. El Cuchillo gripped the shovel with both hands like a weapon and said bitterly, "No guard duty tonight. It's too dangerous. We'll sleep in the bunkers."

Jackson sighed deeply. He was nervous, his stomach tight. The pot in which he had brewed tea was warm. He lifted it and poured more into his cup. The tea tasted good, settling in his stomach.

Luis squatted beside a bucket and washed Sixto's blood from his hands. Two figures approached through the darkness. It was El Cuchillo with Trini. "He found where the *cabrones* were," El Cuchillo said grimly.

"They had horses," Trini said.

"*Donde van*?" Luis asked anxiously.

"Gone. They left quickly, *los cobardes*." Trini said, and spat. "We'll pick up the trail in the morning."

"I'm going with you," Jackson blurted.

Trini squinted. "You know how to ride?"

"Well enough."

Trini looked at El Cuchillo, who shrugged. "It's up to you. Just track them."

Trini nodded at Jackson. "*Bueno*. Be ready at dawn."

※28※

Tierra Amarilla

The next morning's air was cool in the shadows of the tall pines as the sun steadily climbed. Jackson and Trini had been riding steadily for three hours. Jackson relaxed in the saddle, closing his eyes occasionally as the steady swaying motion of the bay mare lulled him. They waited for a couple cars to pass before crossing the highway and riding to a narrow trail through the trees. They crested a hill and a glass-smooth pond opened before them. "We'll stop here," Trini said, dismounting quickly and leading his horse to the edge of the water. Jackson followed. The horses sniffed the water, splashed it with their muzzles, then drank deeply. "Horses first, humans second," Trini said with a smile.

The lake was still, reflecting clouds and the blue sky like a mirror. At the far side, a small fish jumped, rippling the surface. Two birds of prey, hawks he guessed, circled overhead. His butt ached and would be sore the next day. Gripping his left shoulder, he worked his arm in a circle. There was a dull pain where he had landed when the horse bucked him off at first. He felt foolish that he'd left his cell phone on. When it rang, the horse had spooked. Jackson stooped to fill his canteen with fresh water. He was as thirsty as the horses and lifted the canteen and drank. Jackson tied the reins to the trunk of a thin tree and sat on a cushion of pine needles at the base of a large ponderosa.

Trini handed him a plastic bag of beef jerky. "Chew slowly," Trini advised, then inhaled the fragrant, pine-scented air. "God's country," he said, gazing the pond. A soft wind hissed through the high branches. Jackson looked up. The sun was high. He checked his watch: 11:13.

"Where are we?"

"Hanson's ranch," Trini said, chewing.

"Glad you know where we're going."

"I used to guide for him." Trini motioned to the pond. "This is one of his trout ponds. Some big ones in there. He keeps it stocked, with the help of his friends at the Wildlife Department."

Jackson fingered another piece of dried meat from the bag. It had been soaked in chile sauce and was hot. He bit off a piece and chewed. He was hungry.

Soon they were back in the saddle. Trini, with Jackson close behind, reined his horse off the trail and into the woods, winding between trees. The trees were more dense here, the forest more silent. Trini stopped and pointed. Twenty yards beyond was a high chain-link fence topped by three strands of barbed wire.

"What the hell?" Jackson exclaimed.

Trini smiled. "Hanson's. He's got a fence to keep his elk in. Or so he says. In some places it's not so high that they can't jump over."

"I thought Hanson's was some kind of ranch resort."

"It is. A private game preserve. He shoots trophy elk year round."

"Out of season?"

"If you own the elk, you can shoot them anytime. This fence was built across the migration route. But the elk don't read maps, you know. That Johnson Wildlife Area, that's where most of them winter, that's their calving area. They head up to the high country in the summer, right along here. Now if the herds migrate onto Hanson's preserve, who's to know?"

Trini turned his horse and began to ride slowly along the fence line. After ten minutes he stopped and pointed. Half a dozen doe elk stared from behind it, heads erect, ears perked, black eyes glistening. They quickly stepped away, disappearing into forest. "There's a buck or two nearby, you can be sure." They walked their horses along the fence perimeter in silence until they came to a large gate secured with a thick chain and padlock.

Trini spoke quietly. "In the spring when the elk are hungry, whole herds might just come in here if someone was to put down a few bales of alfalfa and open a gate." He shrugged. "Who knows?"

"It must have cost him a fortune to build this fence," Jackson said.

"Sure," Trini said. "But then he makes a fortune. Each one of the elk is worth thousands. Hanson charges people ten thousand or twenty thousand dollars to come here for a weekend. He guarantees them a trophy elk." Dismounting, Trini took a small knife from his pocket and fiddled with the lock until it sprang open. He swung the gate just wide enough for the horses to pass through. Trini closed the gate behind them and hung the chain and padlock back in place, leaving it unlocked, "just in case we need to get out quick."

They followed an indistinct path through the trees, the remains of a logging road. Trini put a finger to his lips, signaling to Jackson to be quiet. They tied their horses to a tree and Trini whispered, "Follow me, but stay low."

Careful not to step on dead branches, they paused at the edge of the timber, crouching behind trees. There was a wide, low meadow about 1,000 yards across. At the bottom were two of Hanson's tan Hummers parked nose to nose, doors open. Two robust, white-haired men dressed in crisp, camouflaged hunting gear, awkwardly hefted rifles. They looked like over-sized mannequins from a sports store. Hanson talked and gestured. Three women in tight tan shorts, photo vests and tan hiking boots emerged from the Hummers. One handed Hanson a cellular telephone. A couple of cowboys on horseback rode up the valley toward the group. They stopped at the Hummers and talked for a moment with Hanson, who motioned to them into the woods. They rode off quickly, disappearing into the forest on the far side of the meadow. "Watch this," Trini whispered.

"Is that what you did for Hanson?" Jackson whispered.

Trini shook his head. "I took people up into the mountains on horseback. We'd really track the elk. Not this. This is a bunch of bullshit."

The hunters occasionally lifted the rifles to their shoulders, pointing blindly at the forest. After about ten minutes, the hunters had grown bored and restless, and sipped from cocktail glasses, which the women replenished. Occasionally one of the women would sidle up to a man and hug him. Suddenly Hanson motioned and waved to the distance. The hunters hastily put their drinks down and grabbed their rifles.

Three bull elk emerged from the forest, antlers high, their eyes turning toward the danger they sensed as doe elk followed. The elk stopped, transfixed and bunched together, confused at the sudden confrontation with humans. Several shots rang out and two of the bull elk fell. The third male sprang forward and disappeared into the timber. Then one of the fallen struggled up and ran off unsteadily while the other lay on its side, lifted its head and pawed at the ground, trying to stand, bellowing in pain. Hanson waved to the two hunters to lower their guns. The cowboys appeared from trees and rode to the fallen elk. One climbed off his horse and used a large pistol to shoot the wounded elk in the head. The bellowing abruptly ceased. The other cowboy rode after the wounded elk.

"Uh, oh," Trini said. A shot rang out behind them.

Jackson jumped.

Trini looked at him, eyes wide with surprise, but motioned for him to stay down. "Aieeee, that was close," Trini said, turning to look over his shoulder. The shot had come from between them and the fence, not far from where Jackson guessed they had left their horses. The cowboy had tracked the elk and shot it. And, he could have stumbled across their horses. The rifle shot undoubtedly spooked them. Trini motioned a retreat.

Jackson took one last look. Hanson was shaking the hands of the two hunters. The cork of a bottle of champagne was popped and it foamed. A woman whooped and danced while holding a champagne glass high. She toasted the kill. Hanson strutted to his Hummer and reached into it for his cell phone. He scanned the woods, concentrating his gaze toward Jackson. Hanson replaced the phone, then lifted field glasses to his eyes. "We're screwed," Trini said, stepping backwards. "We got to get out of here, *pronto!*"

Crouched and in deep brush, they scrambled to their horses. But the horses were gone. Confused, Jackson and Trini stopped.

"Looking for something?"

§

An hour later, Jackson sat anxiously in a low-backed leather chair in Hanson's office. A man in camo gear stood guard, a rifle on his shoulder, a holstered pistol at his hip. Small U.S. flags sat at either corner of Hanson's desk. On the wall was a large military shield of the First Air Cavalry, with its black horse head on a yellow background. Beside it was another shield which read: "Rio Chama Militia," and under that, "Live Free or Die." Crossed rifles and bolts of lightning completed it.

Jackson and Trini had been stripped of their weapons and brought at gunpoint, none too gently, to Hanson's headquarters in one of the outbuildings of the preserve. They had been separated and Trini was somewhere else. The door opened and Hanson strode in, looking agitated. He sat at the desk and fixed his gaze on Jackson, collecting his thoughts. "So how do you like our little operation?"

Jackson shrugged. "You have a strange way of making people feel welcome."

Hanson bristled. "If you wanted a tour, you could have asked."

"I guess we got sidetracked. What'd you do with Trini?"

Hanson scowled. "I'm the one asking the questions." He shook his head in disgust. "Now, tell me what were you doing here?"

"We went for a ride."

Hanson slowly flushed, flexed his jaw muscle. "I'm a very good host, you know. If my guests follow the rules. But you. You and your friend were trespassing. That's a crime." He narrowed his blue eyes.

"Someone was shot yesterday at the protest camp over at the Johnson Wildlife Area. We started following horse tracks and ended up here."

Hanson sat forward suddenly, slowly laced his fingers and smiled wryly. "Sorry to hear that," he said calmly. "I would have figured you'd be smarter than to get mixed up with those people."

"It's my job to get mixed up in other people's business."

"You know what? You're a smart-ass." Hanson pulled a silver, white-handled Colt six-shooter out of his desk and a box of bullets. He held the pistol up and slowly began to put bullets in it. "How do you like this gun?" Hanson asked, not looking at him.

"Don't know much about guns."

"It's a replica of the two pearl-handled pistols that Gen. George Patton wore into battle during W.W.II. Real pearl, too." Hanson admired the weapon, turning it in his hands. "I killed a water buffalo with this once. Put a big hole in its skull." He sighted along the barrel at arm's length, clicked the hammer back with his thumb, then swung his arm until he was pointing at Jackson's nose. After a moment, he put it on the table. "Tell me something," he said softly, "why are you writing about all of this nonsense?"

"Those people have legitimate complaints. They've been here for generations."

"What people think and what is true are two different things. As a journalist, you should know that." He leaned back in his chair. "I got legitimate complaints too, but I don't occupy public land and claim it as my own."

Jackson said nothing.

"So why did you sneak onto my land?"

"We were following tracks, like I said, ended up at your place."

Hanson thought for a moment. "You think I'm involved in this, don't you? And if I was, do you think I'd be so stupid as to shoot someone and not cover my tracks?" His face reddened. "Man, but you got a lot of nerve. You ride onto my land, you trespass, and you interfere with a hunt, which is how I make a living. Then you accuse me of killing someone. I'd say you owe me something. Beginning with an apology."

Jackson swallowed. The last thing he was going to do was apologize. "Well...ah...."

Hanson shook his head in disgust, picked up the pistol again, and turned it in the light. "I suppose you're gonna blame it on your buddy, ol' Trini. He's the one who got you into this, isn't he?"

"It seemed like a good day for a ride," Jackson said, shifting in his chair.

Holding the pistol with both hands now, Hanson pointed it between Jackson's eyes and squinted as he sighted down the barrel. "Okay, Mister Journalist. I got a way you can make this up to me," he said through clenched teeth. "I want you to write a story about me."

Jackson's hands felt cold. Hanson was crazy if he thought he could force anyone to print a story about him. Jackson shook his head. "I'm just writing about I see and what people say. There's not much more to it."

"Gee, the newspaper doesn't seem to have much problem printing your stories about the protesters. Aren't you supposed to get both sides of the story?" He grinned behind the pistol, revealing a full set of teeth. With another gesture by Hanson, the guard left the room, returning with the saddlebags which he dropped at Jackson's feet. "Get out your notebook," he ordered.

Jackson sighed, then slowly unbuckled the bag and pawed through it. Everything was there. He opened a notebook to a blank page. "Okay," Jackson said with deep resignation.

※29※

Santa Fe

Hanson's was the usual militia philosophy: this country was going to hell in a hand basket, but not everyone was going down without a fight. The national decline had begun in the 1930s with the commie-pinko socialists and the New Deal. The 1940s and 1950s reversed the trend, but then came the Sixties and the Hippies. Environmentalism was a plot to destroy capitalism. Stop logging to save a bird? Profits from public lands were stymied by pointy-headed liberals, all for the sake of a few little critters. As he talked, his face reddened then paled and reddened again.

"The goddamn world has gone crazy," Hanson yelled, waving his pistol above his head. "Well, some of us aren't going to roll over and play dead. We're not going to take it. We've armed ourselves against the inevitable collapse of this once-glorious nation. When that happens, and it will very soon, then only the strong will survive. And you can bet your bottom dollar that when the dust settles, we'll still be here."

Hanson paused, then exhaled seemingly to pull himself together, and spoke softly. "But it's getting bad. The government goons are killing those who arms themselves with anything stronger than a pop gun. Hell, look at Ruby Ridge. A goddamn innocent man, his son and wife shot. Then Waco. If Waco wasn't a wake-up call, nothing is."

Jackson shifted uneasily in his chair and wrote quickly to catch up.

Hanson looked out the window, pensive. "According to the government, anyone who believes in individual freedom is a threat. And that, my friend, is communism. But we're not about to take any of that shit." He turned and glared at Jackson. "We're armed and we're prepared to die. That scares the hell out of them."

“Those protesters hate the government as much as you,” Jackson interjected. “The government took their land. They want it back. They’re armed and they’re ready to die for it.” Jackson held his breath.

“It’s bullshit.” Hanson slammed his meaty hand on the desk. He grimaced, gritted his teeth and shook his head. He sighed, then spoke in a whisper. “You just don’t get it. It’s like you’re brainwashed. It’s totally and completely different, for Christ’s sake. They’re just stealing land that’s not theirs.”

Jackson jabbed the air with his pen. “Long ago, their ancestors were given that land by Mexico in exchange for settling the area.”

Hanson shrugged and held out a hand. “Who the hell was the Mexican government to do that?” Silence hung in the air. “Look, just because some people were not smart enough to hang onto what they had, does not mean the rest of us have to suffer. Now if they want to buy the land back from the state or exchange it, that’s different.” He put the gun on the desk and leaned forward on his elbows. “I got this land fair and square with hard, cold cash. They don’t have the money. So, they’re trying to take it with guns. That way they don’t have to pay for it. And, because of you guys in the bleeding-heart media, they could win. Sway public sentiment.” Hanson stood and leaned forward on his fists. “They’re freeloaders, nothing but leeches on the free enterprise system. They’re pests that need to be exterminated before they suck America dry.” He hissed out his final sentence.

“So that’s why the old shepherd was killed?” Jackson said.

Hanson flushed, but said nothing. Hanson would never admit to anything even if he had pulled the trigger, Jackson thought. “And the guy last night?”

“Maybe they had enemies neither of us will ever know about?” Hanson said, unable to control a small grin.

Jackson sighed and lowered his notebook. “Those land grant people,” he said quietly, “they aren’t the only ones living off the public land, are they?”

“You son-of-a-bitch! What are you saying?”

“Your elk winter on and calve in that state wildlife area. And you make a pile of money from those elk.”

“That’s crap. That’s a goddamn stinking lie. Why do you think we built those high fences? We have our own breeding program here.”

“Those big fences have gates.”

"You idiot. The gates are for maintenance only," he yelled. Hanson grabbed his pearl-handled pistol again.

Jackson fell silent. He folded his notebook. "Well, I think I've got all I need."

For a long moment, Hanson stared at Jackson, who did not know if he was going to leave the office alive. "Now I want you to listen and listen closely. Then you're going to write up what I have to say," Hanson said. "After that, one of my men will take you both where ever you want. And, I want to see it in print."

§

Jackson wrote it quickly like a long letter to the editor, a diatribe filled with all of Hanson's favorite phrases. Hanson scrolled through it on Jackson's laptop and nodded approvingly. "Not bad," he said, then smiled warmly. "You could be one of us."

Jackson shook his head. "I doubt it."

Hanson scowled. "Now send it."

Jackson sent the story as an attachment to an email he sent to Ed, saying he'd call later, but was with a local militia leader who opposed the land grant protest group. He then called Stacy.

"Where the hell are you?" Stacy yelled. "The shit has hit the fan, Jackson. Your buddy there, El Cuchillo, has taken a cop hostage. The police and national guard are there in spades this time."

"You're kidding!"

"No, I'm not. Look Jackson, this is our story. Don't let me down."

"All right, all right," Jackson said.

"Where are you now?"

With Hanson looking over his shoulder, Jackson explained his situation. Stacy was silent. "We won't print that."

"Look, it's my ass that's on the line here, not yours," Jackson said. "Perhaps we can dispense with some of the sanctimonious bullshit on the editorial page for just a moment?" Jackson sighed. "Just tell them this piece is a unique perspective on the situation and will expand the on-going debate."

"Send it," Stacy said. "Tell Hanson we need to look it over first. But a letter to the editor shouldn't be a problem."

§

The Hummers were roomy, ugly, mega-toys. The driver, an overgrown teenager in camo gear, wore headphones attached to a portable CD player on his lap. Jackson could hear a strong beat, and guessed it was hip-hop as the driver bobbed his head to the beat.

El Cuchillo's camp was a recurring nightmare. National Guard command center tents were set up in the pastures where they had been days earlier. Green military helicopters waited silently, like giant grasshoppers ready to spring. Jackson checked his watch. Ten minutes after five. The Hummer bounced up the rutted dirt road and stopped at a state patrolman with his hand up. He leaned in the driver's window. The driver slid his earphones down his neck.

"You part of this operation?" the cop asked.

The driver laughed. "No, but it looks like a hell of a party."

The police officer scowled. "Turn it around. This is official police business here."

"Wait," Jackson said, handing him his press pass. "I've been covering this story for weeks. My vehicle is up there."

The cop took the card, glanced at it and handed it back. "All right. Park here. This is for press parking."

"I let you off here?" the driver asked.

"You got that right," Jackson said as he grabbed the saddle bags. "Thanks."

The Hummer backed up and drove down the road, dust trailing. To Jackson's right, three television station helicopters had settled in the field. The television vans were back, but there seemed to be more. Crews were setting up. A group of reporters crowded around Vince Taylor near one of the TV vans. Jackson pulled out his notebook and hustled toward them.

There were some familiar faces and some new ones. One of the out-of-towners, a square-jawed man in a fashionably faded jeans jacket, lifted his hand.

"Jack Thompson, *New York Times*. Just to clarify, you're telling us you have no plans to storm the trailer?"

"No need to," Taylor said confidently. "Like I said, we're negotiating right now. We want to avoid bloodshed."

"What are their demands?" Thompson asked.

"Sorry, can't discuss that."

Equipment on their shoulders, cameramen jostled each other as they pushed forward. "Excuse me, excuse me." A stocky redhead with curly hair rammed his camera through the crowd, banging a photographer, who shoved back fiercely, pushing the television cameraman to his knees. He struggled to his feet, red-faced and cursing, and shoved his camera into the photographer. A reporter stepped in front of the photographer, holding up his hand. "Easy, easy," he said.

"A bunch of goddam goats," Taylor muttered. "Like I was saying, we are negotiating the release of the hostage."

"What's it gonna take?" asked a tanned, sandy-haired man. "Stan Parker with CNN."

"I can't divulge that," Taylor said. "But I can tell you this. We plan to get the officer out of this alive."

"Is Chief Woodward negotiating?" Brock asked.

Taylor nodded. "Look, that's all I can give you now. I'll let you know of developments as they happen. Thanks." A couple of reporters barked out questions, but Taylor waved them off, climbed into a police cruiser, and drove off.

Jackson fished through the saddlebags and found the notebook he wanted. He flipped through the pages for the number of El Cuchillo's cellular phone. Putting distance between himself and the others, he punched in the number. The line was busy. He spotted Brock. Jackson needed some fast catching up. "Donna, what the hell happened?"

She shaded her eyes from the late afternoon sun. "Supposedly El Cuchillo took a Rio Chama County sheriff deputy hostage. A guy named Lucero, I think." She turned through the pages of her notebook. "Yeah, Anthony Lucero. He and a state patrolman came here this morning to investigate the shooting yesterday evening."

"Yeah. A guy named Sixto Hernandez."

"He's at University Hospital in critical condition."

Jackson shook his head. "Damn."

"Anyway, El Cuchillo got the jump on Lucero, grabbed his gun, then took him hostage. The state patrolman backed off, then called for help." Brock gestured to the police and military. "He got some."

"Even CNN and the *New York Times*. It's getting to be real news now, I guess."

"They think it's another Waco. But no one's up there except El Cuchillo and Lucero."

"I think he's got Manuelito with him," Jackson said.

"You sure?"

"The kid was there early this morning. His mother, Antonia, went to the Espanola hospital last night with Sixto and his wife when he was shot. Did she come back?"

"Don't know. Why were you here this morning?"

"I went for a horseback ride. It's a long story."

The CNN crew was in position with a camera on a tripod and a fuzzy sleeve covering the microphone hanging from the end of a telescoping boom. Parker looked in a hand-held mirror, combed his hair, then sprayed it. Jackson paused within earshot. Parker fitted an earpiece in place, then cleared his throat and looked at the camera.

"Yeah, I can hear you...yeah. It's fine...yep. Ready anytime you are." He checked a small monitor on a folding chair beside him. After a moment, he took a deep breath and cleared his throat, eyes intent on the camera. "No, Joyce, this is not another Waco, but believe me, the scene is just as tense. A group of armed people laying claim to an old Mexican land grant have taken a county sheriff deputy hostage. He'd being held in that small camp over there." Parker turned and gestured toward the camp. "As you can see, the police have it surrounded." Parker paused, staring at the camera. "As far as we know, the hostage is unharmed. The police say they are negotiating for his release." He paused again. "Certainly, Joyce. We'll keep you updated." Parker looked at the camera, then at the monitor, and groaned. "God. All this way for fifteen stinking seconds."

Jackson's cell phone beeped. He pulled it from his coat pocket and walked away.

"Where the hell have you been?"

"Who is this?"

"Taylor. I don't have much time to explain. Things are not going well here. El Cuchillo wants to talk with you, directly."

"I've seen this movie before," Jackson said.

"Sorry buddy."

"Taylor, what the hell can I do that you can't?"

"We've got Antonia here, but El Cuchillo won't listen to her either."

"So?"

"El Cuchillo wants to issue another communiqué, as he calls it. We're sending a squad car out there get you." Taylor clicked off.

Jackson had a sinking feeling again as he watched a black and white state police cruiser bounce down the road toward him.

※30※

Tierra Amarilla

Antonia stood beside the police communication van, her eyes sunken and her face fallen. She seemed to have aged overnight. "Good to see you," she said, stepping back and raking her fingers through her disheveled hair. "El Cuchillo has stopped talking... to them and to me. I don't know what to do. Manuelito's all right, but El Cuchillo doesn't want to let him go. The police say Manuelito is a hostage too, but he's not."

Jackson shook his head sadly.

"Over here," Taylor yelled. Jackson walked to the open door of the police van. Woodward pulled off his headphones. His face contorted.

"That son of a bitch wants safe passage to Mexico. I can't do that. Now the feds are on the way."

"Did you tell him that?" Jackson asked.

"He doesn't trust me."

"Should he?"

Woodward grimaced.

"So you want me to be your errand boy again?" Jackson asked.

"I don't want you to do shit. El Cuchillo asked for you, not me. He's got a hostage in there, and I want that deputy out. Alive. You got that?"

Jackson nodded.

"Tell El Cuchillo I can get him to the Chama airport. But that's it. After that, he deals with the feds. Even if he does get to Mexico, he'll be arrested the minute he steps off the plane. He's better off letting Lucero go and giving himself up."

They looked at each other in silence. A telephone rang softly.

"It's ATF," a technician said, handing Woodward the phone.

Cupping his hand over the mouthpiece, he waved at Jackson to leave.

Jackson got up and stepped out.

Antonia waited beside the police van with Taylor, who puffed nervously on a cigarette.

"Is there anything that will convince him to give it up?" Jackson asked her.

Antonia bit her lip. Her arms hugged her chest as she slowly shook her head. "If I knew...."

Jackson looked toward the pale green trailer. "Here goes nothing. Tell them I'm going in," he said to Taylor.

"They know already," Taylor said.

Jackson made his way between the half-dozen police vehicles at the entrance to the camp. The protest posters were now ripped and torn, flapping in the breeze. No man's land is a lonely place, he thought, his stomach knotting. He passed his truck, Trini's horse trailer, and the now cold campfire where he hesitated, then stepped forward and knocked on the trailer door.

"Come in," El Cuchillo called out. Jackson turned the door handle.

Inside, Lucero and El Cuchillo sat at the kitchen table, both with a cup of coffee as if it were a friendly visit and Lucero had come to chat. A .45 automatic pistol and a cellular phone were on the table beside El Cuchillo's right hand. Lucero looked up at Jackson with a sheepish grin. Jackson recognized him as the deputy who had investigated Ariel's assault. Small world, he thought. The table pushed into Lucero's protruding belly.

"How you doing?" Jackson asked Lucero.

Lucero struggled for an answer. "I'm okay."

"We met before," Jackson said casually. Lucero was confused. "You investigated an assault on my girlfriend in Ojo Caliente about a month ago."

"That's possible," Lucero said.

No shit, Jackson thought. He let it drop then looked at El Cuchillo. "It's pretty tense out there."

El Cuchillo stiffened. "Of course. This is war."

"The feds are involved now. It's a different ball game."

"The federal government has always been involved. They created this mess and they can clean it up."

"It ain't gonna happen. You know that."

El Cuchillo's jaw flexed. He looked exhausted. "This is the way it has to come down," he said. "There's no...other...way."

"Lawsuits," Jackson said. "Go to court to get the land back. You've got lots of public sympathy on your side now. Don't lose it."

El Cuchillo shook his head impatiently. "*Dinero*," he said, rubbing the fingertips of one hand together. "It takes money."

"Anything's better than this."

"No sheep. No land. No pride." He looked imploringly at Jackson and shook his head.

"You want to be a martyr?"

"Somebody must stand up and fight." He held his meaty fist up and shook it at Jackson like he was going to smash him in the face.

"There's no easy way out of this now," Jackson said, trying to sound as patient as possible.

"I'll get out. Anthony an' me have been talkin'. He's gonna help me get to Mexico. Is the plane ready yet?"

Jackson shrugged. "I don't know. They told me you had a statement."

El Cuchillo sighed, dropped his gaze to his coffee cup, then picked up the pistol and pointed it at Jackson. "Just take this down, mister reporter."

Jackson shook his head and pulled his notebook from his back pocket and his pen from his shirt.

"Now write this. *El Cooperativo del Valle* has seized this land in protest of more than a hundred years of injustice that has been perpetrated by the government of the United States." Jackson jotted as fast as he could. "Two of our people have been shot, one of them killed. But we have harmed no one. The guilty go unpunished. The innocent continue to suffer."

"Slow down," Jackson said.

"I have demanded safe passage to Mexico where I will be welcomed with opened arms." El Cuchillo sounded strangely confident. "I am an example to others of the continuing struggle for freedom and justice for people of color everywhere." He paused. "Now read it back to me."

Jackson did.

"Now go," El Cuchillo said.

"One question," Jackson said. "Where's Manuelito?"

"Manuelito," El Cuchillo called out. Manuelito came out from the bedroom.

He looked sullen and wore a t-shirt, camo pants, and high top canvas shoes.

El Cuchillo nodded. "Now he is a young soldier. Tell Woodward I am waiting," El Cuchillo said arrogantly.

Jackson stopped at the door and looked at the anxious Lucero and again at El Cuchillo. "Adios," he said softly.

Outside the air was warm. A breeze stirred the trees and shadows flickered on the ground. Dozens armed police stood ready at the perimeter fence. The place was surrounded. They would not go home empty-handed, Jackson thought. His shoulder and neck ached as he walked down the road.

§

Jackson read the statement to Woodward.

"That guy just doesn't get it, does he?" Woodward said.

"No, you don't get it," Jackson said, his stomach knotting. "Not everyone stands and salutes the flag at the crack of dawn because not everyone in this country gets a fair shake. He's just fighting back. In his own way."

"It's wrong," Woodward said with contempt. "You're no better than the rest of them."

"El Cuchillo wants to know when his plane is going to be ready."

"A couple hours."

"Better tell him. I'm going outside to give out his statement."

Woodward yelled to Taylor. "Get this guy out of here."

At the cattle guard down the road where the news media was gathered, Jackson and Taylor climbed out of the cruiser.

"How come he gave you the statement?" Thompson asked.

"Because El Cuchillo knows me. I've been covering this story for weeks. Where the hell have you been?"

Taylor lifted a hand. "Hold on. Jackson will read a statement from El Cuchillo so you all can have it."

Thompson scowled, noisily flipping the pages his notebook.

Jackson cleared his throat and read. Cameras rolled and reporters scribbled, some holding tape recorders.

"Is that it?" Thompson asked.

Jackson stared at him.

Thompson turned to Taylor. "Are you guys going to give him a plane or not?"

"All I can say is that we're negotiating."

"Do you deny it?"

"Can't do that either."

The reporters groaned.

"El Cuchillo has asked to be helicoptered to Chama where he will be put on a private plane and flown to Mexico City," Jackson blurted. "He expects to be granted asylum there."

"Asylum?" Thompson asked.

Begrudgingly, Jackson explained. "He says he's a citizen of Mexico because the United States violated the Treaty of Guadalupe Hidalgo when this region became part of the United States."

"The treaty of what?"

"Gua-da-lu-pe Hi-dal-go."

"How do you spell that?"

"Jesus H. Christ," Jackson said, looking into the distance.

"What was the mood in the trailer?" Thompson asked.

"Somber. Just like you'd expect."

"How was Lucero?" Brock asked.

"He's had better days."

"What does that mean?"

Jackson smiled. "Scared shitless."

§

Jackson sat in the passenger seat of Brock's Volvo. He looked at the screen of his laptop, tugged at his mustache and read what he had written:

> EL VALLE, NEW MEXICO – A sheriff deputy and an eleven-year-old boy were held hostage by a land grant protester inside a trailer here while outside a small army of police with helicopters and high-powered weapons waited for their release.
>
> This deadly standoff showed no signs of change late Thursday as El Cuchillo, the self-styled leader of an armed land grant protest

over grazing rights, demanded safe passage to Mexico for himself and Sheriff Deputy Anthony Lucero of Espanola, who was taken hostage.

He continued to write, tapping the keys of his laptop furiously. An hour later, after getting weak signal, Jackson transmitted the story via his cell phone.

Stacy loved it.

"Exclusive, don't forget."

"That's what you're paid for. What's next?"

"They're talking about getting him an airplane at the Chama airport. I can't say what's going to happen. When something does, I'll call. But the story should stand for the time being." As Jackson hung up, a couple of white, four-wheel drive Ford Explorers rolled past him and bounced over the cattle guard after a police officer waved them through and barreled up the road to the camp.

§

By seven o'clock in the evening, reporters and cameramen were restless. Most had gone live for the six o'clock news. Now the wait began. The sun hung low in the sky, sending long shafts of golden light through the trees, across the fields. Jackson wondered if Woodward was still negotiating. Jackson got out of Brock's Volvo, leaned against the grill, and tapped in the numbers into his mobile phone.

"Taylor here."

"It's Jackson. What's happening?"

"Good thing you called. Antonia wants to talk to you. She's here with me outside the communications van."

Antonia came on. "I'm afraid for Manuelito," she pleaded. "Can you get him out of there?" Jackson's stomach tightened.

"You're his mother. Why don't *you* talk to El Cuchillo? Tell him to let Manuelito go."

"El Cuchillo won't listen to me anymore."

Jackson paused. "So what do you have in mind?"

"Deliver a written guarantee from Woodward for safe passage and bring Manuelito out."

"Shit." Jackson fell silent. "What does Woodward say?"

"Here he is," Antonia said.

Woodward came on the line. "Jackson, help us get Manuelito out. We'll deal with Lucero separately."

"How?" Jackson asked.

"We're writing down the terms, just so there's no misunderstanding. It's conditional on Manuelito being released. You walk him out."

Jackson sighed.

§

Woodward handed Jackson a printout. "Here it is." Woodward pulled off his sunglasses and massaged the bridge of his nose. Two other heavily armed officers, each husky and wearing black nylon jackets monogrammed with ATF, looked at him blankly. Jackson felt a penetrating chill in his body. His stomach ached.

"I give this to El Cuchillo. He gives me Manuelito. We walk out."

Woodward nodded.

Without speaking, Jackson turned and walked slowly up the road to the trailer. He wondered how Lucero was handling all of this as he knocked on the trailer door.

"Come in," a voice said.

Jackson opened the door and stepped inside. Manuelito leaned against the narrow kitchen counter and looked sad and lonely. El Cuchillo and Lucero were still at the table. The air was thick and stifling.

El Cuchillo glanced at Jackson, worry clouding his face. "You got it?" he asked.

Jackson tossed the paper on the table.

El Cuchillo picked it up and read it slowly. "Done," he exhaled, closed his eyes and tilted his head back. After a long moment, El Cuchillo opened his eyes and picked up the .45, pointing it at Jackson. "But there's been a change of plans," he said, pulling back the hammer with his thumb. "Manuelito goes with Lucero. But you stay."

Jackson frowned and swallowed as his stomach soured. "What? I'm not staying! I'm taking Manuelito. That's the deal." Jackson's hands trembled. He jammed them into his jeans. A cold clammy sweat broke out on his forehead.

"Change of plans. Lucero!" El Cuchillo barked. It made the deputy jump. "Take Manuelito out of here."

Lucero slid his puffy belly out of the cramped seat and stood nervously, his dark eyes darting from El Cuchillo, to Jackson, and then to Manuelito.

"Manuelito, go with Anthony here," El Cuchillo said.

Manuelito stood still. Tears filled his eyes. He went to El Cuchillo and wrapped his arms around his neck.

El Cuchillo hugged the boy, then tousled his hair. "Good-bye, *mi hijo*." He looked longingly at Manuelito, wiped a tear from Manuelito's cheek, then his face hardened. He waved his gun at Lucero. "Take him."

Lucero took the boy's hand, opened the door and disappeared. El Cuchillo used a finger to push aside the curtain slightly and watch them walk away.

"Why me?" Jackson asked, his throat tight, his voice breaking.

"You're a better hostage. You're a gringo."

Jackson's mind raced. "Did Woodward know about this?"

El Cuchillo nodded. "It was an exchange of prisoners."

"Shit," Jackson groaned, as the betrayal gripped his chest. His legs felt weak. There was nothing he could do about it now. "What else don't I know?"

"I hope you like Mexico. We're going together."

El Cuchillo really believed that, Jackson thought. "Why do you trust them?"

"Shut up," El Cuchillo said.

El Cuchillo picked up the cell phone and punched in a number. "Send the helicopter now." He clicked it off, stood, and slipped the phone into the pocket of his hunting vest.

A few minutes later, a helicopter thudded overhead.

"Turn around," he said.

Jackson complied.

El Cuchillo stood behind him, then hooked Jackson's neck in the crook of his big left arm and pulled him back. Jackson choked and felt the cold steel of the gun barrel at the back of his head. El Cuchillo pushed it hard against him. "Don't fight me. Understand?"

Jackson used a foot to kick open the trailer door. They stepped clumsily to the ground. It was much cooler outside as Jackson strained to scan the scene. Police waited behind their cruisers, rifles pointed at them. El Cuchillo pushed him forward. They walked haltingly for a few steps, pausing near the campfire. Jackson's body quivered and his legs buckled slightly, but El Cuchillo jerked him up, choking him.

"Stand up," El Cuchillo grunted.

The helicopter thudded above the police line, blowing dust and grit everywhere. It slowly descended toward them, hovering above the field between the camp and the road.

A searing white pain surged through Jackson's body from his left thigh. He felt his leg collapse as he slipped to the ground at the sharp crack of a rifle shot, and was suddenly free of El Cuchillo's grip. Jackson writhed on the ground and grasped his left thigh with both hands. It was warm and wet. "Jesus," Jackson moaned. He opened his eyes. El Cuchillo stood above him holding his pistol, dumbfounded.

Shots erupted like a string of fire crackers, popping and thumping into El Cuchillo's chest as he staggered backwards. His pistol flew into the air as he fell to the ground with a heavy thud and a deep groan, dust rising around him.

※31※

Santa Fe

Jackson drifting in and out of consciousness as he lay between crisp, clean sheets in the hospital bed and breathed the sterile, antiseptic air. His mind was a jumble of confused images. His stomach knotted as he imagined El Cuchillo death in slow motion, again and again, falling behind him to the ground. The medication, the pain killers, left him untethered. Even with his eyes open, reality felt like a dream. The dull ache in his left leg was like the crashing of waves of an unsettled sea. The pain rose slowly and steadily to a crescendo, then subsided into a weak throb. He slipped his hand down to his heavily-bandaged left thigh. He tried to move the leg slowly, but stopped as a sharp pain surged up his left side. He groaned.

Thanks to the pain, he was awake now. His mouth felt dry, another benefit of the medication, and he turned his head slowly and focused on the yellow plastic pitcher on the tray table. It probably had water, but he was too tired to reach for it.

El Cuchillo came to his mind again. They had killed him. In cold blood. But they shot me first to get me out of the way and give them a clear shot. They didn't need to do that. Trigger happy bastards. Who had ordered the shooting? The feds or the state? What did it matter?

Probably Woodward and his boys were so damn anxious show the feds some New Mexico style justice, the mere suggestion of shooting El Cuchillo was all they needed. Shoot first, ask questions later. Step out of line: bam! Get in the way: bam! Jackson managed a hard swallow. El Cuchillo was not a real danger to them and they knew it. One gun against fifty? The cops weren't afraid. They were trigger happy. But this was not the end of the protest. No. It was far from over.

The door to his semi-private room opened slightly and Ariel's face appeared. She smiled at him weakly. "You're awake?"

Jackson managed a smile. She pushed open the door, quietly closed it behind her, went to his bedside and kissed him on the forehead. He inhaled her earthy, perfumed air, felt the brush of her hair on his face.

"How are you doing?" she whispered, smoothing his hair and slipping her hand behind his head.

"Okay, I guess," he said with a pained voice, then glanced at the yellow pitcher. "Can you pour me a glass of water?" She reached for it and poured him a glass. He lifted his head, but was too horizontal to drink.

"Here." She found the control on the bed and pushed a button. The bed clunked and the head end rose slowly. Sitting up, Jackson took the cup, swallowed deeply, and held it out for more. She poured. "How's your leg feel?"

"It hurts. But only if I try to move it."

She sighed sympathetically and massaged the back of his neck. "Poor baby." Her light blue eyes mellowed and watered. She dropped her gaze to the sheets and blinked, her eyes tearing. She wiped them quickly with a finger. "Oh shit. I wasn't going to cry." She laughed haltingly. "You don't need me crying at your bed."

"It's all right." Jackson put a hand on her shoulder, pulling her close. She nestled her face against his neck. He moved his hand slowly up and down her back. She lay her head on his shoulder and he felt her warm breath. Her tears moistened his thin hospital gown.

He let her cry, but didn't quite know for whom or what the tears were shed. For him, for her, for the whole mess? It didn't matter. He felt sadness well up in him again, thickening his throat, and he felt he was choking. Then his chin quivered and his eyes watered. He couldn't hold it back any more. He held her tightly and cried.

Moments later, feeling burdened by the overwhelming futility of it all, he sensed a void of reason and common sense, like he was standing on the edge of a cliff with nothing below but emptiness. His left thigh throbbed badly again and he felt a wave of pain. "Can you reach me those pills?"

Ariel sighed and reached. She shook out a couple of pills and she handed them to him with a cup of water. It was more pain killer than he probably needed, but he didn't care. Ariel looked at him again, now more calm and clear. She cleared her throat. "The reason I came here was to tell you that I'm leaving." She held her breath as the words hung in the air.

Jackson searched her face. The words stunned him. "You're leaving?"

She slowly nodded, blinking watery eyes. "Damn. There they are again." She reached for a tissue and dabbed her eyes. "I never should have come to New Mexico in the first place. Nothing has worked out. It's time for me to go back to California. I miss my friends. I miss my parents. I want to go home."

"It's okay, Ariel."

She waited for him to say something else, but he had nothing to say. "Thanks," she whispered after a long pause. She leaned close and her warm, soft lips lingered on his. She slowly sat up and smoothed his hair again. "The doctor says you're going to be all right. It was a clean shot. A flesh wound. It'll heal just fine."

"A clean shot? It'll heal? Jesus H. Christ." Jackson looked away. "Idiots." He looked back at Ariel. "How are you getting home?"

"I've packed my Saab. It's in the parking lot. I'm leaving from here."

"You're serious, then."

She nodded. "You'll be okay." She reached inside her purse and pulled out one of Jackson's notebooks and a pen. She flipped it open and scribbled something on it. "Here. My number and address. Call me."

Jackson looked at what she had written. It was her name, address and phone number, below which she wrote "Love, Ariel," and over the "i" she had drawn a little heart. Jackson figured that meant something, but wasn't sure what.

"Where's my truck and my computer?"

"The truck is still at the camp I guess. I brought everything else back to your place. It's all on the kitchen table."

"How long have I been here?"

"A couple of days. You have lots of phone calls. That's why I brought your phone and notebook."

"Thanks." He held her hand.

"I better go now," she said, "while I still can." She hugged him tightly. He liked the way she felt, and he knew he would remember that and would miss it. She rose and looked at him one last time, her eyes wet again. "Good-bye." She turned and left, closing the door softly.

§

Jackson drifted into an unsettled sleep and awoke feeling more tired than before. He looked around the room. Ariel was long gone. But he could have dreamt that. He remembered the notebook and it was still there on the tray table. Theirs had been a kind of unreal relationship anyway, he thought. He didn't really know how he felt about Ariel. It didn't matter now. She was gone. He would be okay. Only the hole inside him felt just a little bigger. That's all.

The door opened again and an old woman came in wearing an aqua-green nylon coat and a puffy paper cap, the kind they wear during surgery. With hunched shoulders, she shuffled along in paper-covered shoes. She clumped the tray on the stand, not looking at him, and mumbled something that Jackson understood to mean lunch. She glanced at him quickly from dark, milky eyes set in a face wrinkled like a dried apple. The odor of soup rose from the tray.

Jackson was struck with a mixture of nausea and hunger. He didn't know which would win. He pressed the control button and the mattress lifted him up. He reached for the tray. A watery brown liquid sloshed inside a white plastic bowl, and in that floated a collection of what might once have been vegetables and meat. He sipped from a spoon. It had little taste, but probably had nourishment. He'd need that. There was also a bowl of yellow macaroni and a wilted salad with a tasteless wedge of tomato.

A television screen hung on the wall. It was big and projected itself into the room. He checked his watch. It was time for the local six o'clock news. He twisted slowly and painfully over to the night stand and grabbed the remote, clicked it on. A blotchy color screen appeared. After some ads, the young and bright-eyed face of a broadcaster came on. Jackson increased the volume when footage of the El Cuchillo camp came on. Jesus.

"Two state police officers, whose names have not been released, have been placed on paid administrative leave in the wake of the killing of a man known as El Cuchillo, the leader of group of Hispanic land grant protesters who demanded grazing rights to a state-owned wildlife area nearby.

"State police say they are conducting an internal investigation into the shooting and refused to comment."

The broadcast cut to Chief Woodward, who said, "I really can't comment. We're conducting an investigation. If we knew the answers now, we wouldn't have to investigate."

"Jesus H. Christ," Jackson muttered.

The young woman's face returned to the screen. "An attorney for the protesters says the group intends to file a wrongful death lawsuit in the case."

His wire-rimmed glasses glinting, Montrose appeared. "This was nothing more than a summary execution," he said, looking at a reporter in the glare of lights. "This was a gross abuse of police powers. This is worse than the George Floyd murder. And the whole world was watching. Are we going to sue? You bet."

The woman's face returned to the screen: "The incident has drawn national attention and sparked outrage from a number of national advocacy groups. Meanwhile, journalist Luke Jackson, who was wounded in the incident, remains in stable but serious condition in a Santa Fe hospital." She turned to another camera. "What's in the weather? Our meteorologist will tell you all about it after these messages."

Jackson's head and his stomach ached. He clicked the television off. I'm stable but serious, he thought. Yeah. That's about right. Serious. Perhaps too serious. He took a deep breath. Life was not getting any simpler. This was not going to be over anytime soon. Ariel had left and now he knew why. She'd had enough and she saw that it was only going to get worse. She'd bailed and with good reason. But still... .

He picked up his telephone and punched the numbers to his voice messaging. Sixteen messages, the mechanical voice said. Okay. Here we go. Jackson held the pen to the notebook and pushed the "1" button. Everyone had called. The Santa Fe and Albuquerque newspapers, the Albuquerque television stations, CNN, the *New York Times*, the *LA Times*, and others, including Montrose, Antonia, Luna, and even Margo. He had a long list of names and numbers to call, but started with Luna. She must be going through hell, he thought. She was in Los Angeles and may have learned on the evening news that her father had been shot.

Jackson dialed and let the phone ring. Luna's message clicked on that she wasn't there, etc. "Hello sweetheart. This is your daddy and I'm calling to tell you that I'm okay and that I'll call you again later...."

"Is that you?" Margo barked, fumbling with the phone, dropping it with a loud clunk.

He groaned and held the phone away from his ear.

"Are you all right? This is Margo."

"I'm alive."

Margo was silent then spoke softly. "There're some people who care for you a great deal. Luna has been worried sick."

"Where is she?"

"She's at her tennis lesson. I thought it would be good to get her mind off you."

"How thoughtful. Tell her to call me. Here in the hospital."

"So what happened?"

"Didn't you see it?"

"Yeah, but how did you get in the middle of it?"

"I was a go-between. Then they took me hostage for a short time. He tried to use me as a shield, but the bastards shot me anyway so they could shoot him."

She was quiet. "That's awful." She was silent again. "How do you feel?"

"I hurt."

"But you're all right?"

"For someone who had his leg shot by a high-powered rifle. Yeah. I guess."

"Well, when you're feeling better, Jim would like to talk to you. He thinks your story has a lot of movie potential."

"Hollywood just doesn't waste a minute, does it? Swoop down on a human tragedy and pick apart the carcass."

"You should know. You're a reporter." She paused. "So, don't call him. I don't care."

"Have Luna call me, okay?"

"I will."

Jackson hung up. He heard a note of sincerity in Margo's voice.

※32※

Santa Fe

Something was touching his hand. Jackson jerked and opened his eyes. Antonia was at the bedside, her hand on his. His sudden awakening surprised her and she sat back, eyes wide, and withdrew her hand.

"Antonia? What...?"

"How are you?" she asked.

He blinked awake. "Ahhh…you came down from El Valle?"

She nodded. He put his hand other hand on top of hers. Her eyes watered and she turned away, choking down a sob. She covered her mouth with a hand to muffle it. It didn't work. Jackson sighed.

"I'm sorry," she said. "I came here to give you some support, not to cry."

"Thanks," he said. "You didn't need to come."

She wiped away her tears.

He closed his eyes and knew his grief had been replaced with remorse. Contempt and anger were on the way.

"When is El Cuchillo going to be buried?"

She drew a deep breath and sat up, wiping her eyes with a tissue. "I don't know. They still have the body."

"Autopsy?"

She nodded. "I don't know when or even if they'll give it back."

"They will." He took her hand again. He went to move his right arm but felt the tug of the intravenous tube and needle stuck in it. The lifeline oozed clear liquids into his blood. "They'll check the bullet holes, try figure out who killed him. They need someone to blame."

She looked at him, puzzled.

"If the public heat gets to be too much, they'll find one of their trigger happy boys and blame him, say he acted without orders, used excessive force. The poor guy will be lucky to be a rent-a-cop for the rest of his life."

Antonia shook her head slowly. Her thick hair was pulled back and tied loosely behind her head. "This whole thing is awful. It just won't end. Those cops were acting on orders. No one can tell me different."

Jackson nodded. "Of course."

Antonia's eyes flared. "They shouldn't have killed him. That was not right."

§

Two days later, Jackson was stir crazy and it no longer made him dizzy to stand. He had moved around a bit, walking on crutches up and down the halls. He smiled as Antonia was there again and pushed the wheelchair into the room.

"I'm being rescued, finally."

She smiled slightly, then scowled. "They're waiting outside," Antonia said. "A group of reporters."

"Now the fun begins," Jackson said.

Antonia wheeled Jackson through the tiled lobby of St. Vincent's Hospital and toward the glare of sunlight. Jackson squinted.

He felt weird, helpless in a wheelchair. He insisted that he could walk out, on his own, on crutches, but the nurses had refused to let him. Hospital rules, they said. Yeah, he thought. That would actually be the hospital's insurance lawyers' rules.

After rolling through the glass doors and into the sunshine, Jackson welcomed the warmth on his face. It felt like he had returned from the dead. He closed his eyes and tilted his head back to take it all in.

"How are you?"

As he opened his eyes, a looming figure was silhouetted against the sun. He squinted. It was Richard Montrose. "Fine. I guess." Montrose held out Jackson's crutches with one hand and then put another under Jackson's arm to help him up. Jackson struggled to stand on his right leg, then balanced himself precariously on the crutches as his left leg throbbed. It would take some adjusting to learn to maneuver with crutches. Two television cameras and four reporters were gathered. Montrose stood to his right and Antonia to his left. A microphone was held out to Jackson.

"First of all," Brock asked, "how are you doing?"

"Thanks, Donna. As good as can be expected. The doctors predict a full recovery."

"So what do you think about what happened?"

"Obviously, I'm not happy about it. It was an abuse of police powers. It was completely unnecessary."

"You were being held hostage. From the video, you were in the grasp of El Cuchillo. It looked like he was going to shoot you."

Jackson shook his head. "I never felt like I was in danger, at least not from El Cuchillo. He was using me as a shield from the police. I think he knew they were going to kill him. As it turns out, he was right."

"So, are you going to sue?" Brock asked.

Jackson turned to Montrose. "I'd better let him answer that."

Montrose handed out stapled copies of a statement. "What you have there is a summary of a suit that was filed in state district court this morning. In it we are seeking $5 million in penalties and damages for the wrongful death of Alfred Lopez, also known as El Cuchillo. We are also asking for two and a half million in the wrongful shooting of Mr. Jackson here, of whom you all know. We contend that the police were completely unjustified in taking the action that they did, that there was no imminent danger to them or anyone else, and excessive force was used resulting in death and injury."

The reporters watched intently, looking at Montrose and flipping the pages.

"The lawsuit is only part of what we want to talk about." Montrose turned to Antonia.

The cameras focused on her. "Because of the national, even international attention on the land grant issue, I was informed today that our congressman, Orlando Romero, has appealed to the president to establish a federal committee to investigate the historic land grant issue. We are encouraging the president to take this step and to name a commission in hopes that the wrongs of the past can be made right. We, *El Cooperativo del Valle*, also pledge our complete cooperation and support of this initiative. We hope that it will have a successful conclusion so that El Cuchillo's death will not have been in vain. But you can also be assured that no matter what happens, we will never give up our struggle for justice. What the police did has only made us more deeply committed than ever."

The reporters stood silently writing and recording. A couple of photographers snapped off some frames as their motor drives whirred.

"The burial of El Cuchillo is this afternoon in El Valle," Antonia said. "You are welcome to attend."

§

Two Advil helped. Jackson could feel the occasional throb of his leg as he leaned on his crutches on the front porch of the weaving shop in El Valle, but the pain no longer reverberated up and down his body. It felt like a *deja vu* moment, as if he'd seen the funeral procession, the somber collection of humanity that shuffled toward him, eyes downcast. Again the doll of the Virgin floated above the throng, some carrying a black gleaming casket held aloft on stout shoulders. Manuelito lead a riderless horse. Antonia walked beside Manuelito, dressed in a long, black gown, hat and veil, like death herself. The slow clop of the horse's hooves drifted on a soft breeze. A couple of reporters were with Jackson on the store's wooden porch. At the foot of the cement steps of the church, a television crew waited, camera mounted on a tripod.

As the procession passed, Jackson moved clumsily off the steps of the porch, carefully lowering himself down and onto the gravel. As the horse passed, he noticed a stout man wearing sunglasses and a blue blazer over clean and pressed blue jeans, walking amidst the procession. It was Romero, the congressman, hands clasped in front of him.

Jackson nodded and hobbled into the procession beside Romero. If Romero had anything, Jackson thought, he had impeccable timing. He had arrived, finally, to help clean up the mess, but it had taken the death of two men to make it all happen. As the procession approached the church, Romero moved from Jackson's right to his left, positioning himself closer to the cameras. Jackson shook his head slowly. Romero straightened up as he passed the television cameras, then at the bottom of the church steps, paused and held a hand out to Jackson, steadying Jackson has he pushed himself up, one step at a time.

§

A couple of hours later, Romero filled his chair in Antonia's kitchen office of her weaving shop. He had a full jowly face and clear, sympathetic eyes. He looked uncomfortable in the jeans and sat with his elbows on the table as he lifted a pair of meaty hands and held them open. “The little speech I made at the grave side that I would not rest until the people of El Valle found justice, is true. But, I also need to tell you that the situation back in Washington is not good. The president, and I’ve spoken to him personally about this, is sympathetic. But, Congress is not.” Romero scanned the drawn faces of the *consejo*, four weathered faces who’d seen and heard it all. “There are many people back there who are quietly glad that El Cuchillo was killed. They don’t think he had any right to do what he did. They think the same of everyone here today.”

Silence hung in the air. Jackson looked over to Trini, who leaned against the counter and sipped coffee from a white Styrofoam cup.

“But what about the panel, appointed by the president?” Trini asked.

“It’s a step, but it’s just a step,” Romero said. “I’m telling you this because I do not want you to get your hopes up that anything will happen or change very soon.” He looked around the group. “The fact is that U.S. Congress has never been willing to admit the mistakes of the past when it comes to Mexican land grants. All you need to do is to look at all the broken Indian treaties. I frankly don’t think the land grant will ever be returned to the rightful heirs. However, Congress has provided compensation to victims in the past, like those who suffered from atomic testing during the Cold War. I think compensation is our best bet. If we can get that, we’ll be lucky.”

The eyes of the *consejo* were not amused.

“But, the good news is that at least there will be someone looking into the issue. We have to be persistent. I’m willing to go the distance, but I’ll need your help. That’s what I’m asking you for today.”

Several of the *consejo* nodded.

“The president has asked me to recommend some people to the panel. There will be land grant people from Colorado, New Mexico, Arizona, Texas and California. Locally, though, we need someone who knows the issue and can speak well for the people of El Valle.”

All eyes fell on Antonia who was sitting at her desk. She glanced from face to face, then shook her head slightly. “How can I do that and run the wool cooperative, too?”

Romero smiled. “Don’t worry. You’ll be compensated. Your

expenses will be paid. We need your expertise and your passion, Antonia."

She sighed deeply and looked at the floor, thinking.

Later Antonia and Jackson stood on the porch of the weaving store and waved as Romero's black Lincoln town car disappeared down the road. They looked at each other.

"Think we'll ever see him again?" she asked.

Jackson sighed and leaned on his crutches. "Sure. There's publicity to be had here. We'll make sure of that. And probably a few votes."

The setting sun cast long shadows. It was quiet and seemed as if nothing had ever happened. "We still don't know who killed my father," she said.

"It'll come out."

"It just doesn't end, does it," Antonia said quietly.

Jackson took her hand and gave it a gentle squeeze.

READERS GUIDE

1) Why does the main character, Luke Jackson, decide to visit and then stay at the camp of the protesters?
2) What does Jackson do for a living and how long has he been doing it?
3) Who are the protesters?
4) What motivates the protesters to occupy the land?
5) What rights to the land do the protesters claim to have?
6) What do the protesters do for a living?
7) What documents and legalities provide the basis for their claims?
8) A man is murdered in the opening scenes. Who was he and what was his relationship to the land grant protesters?
9) What happened to the original land grant when the states of the Southwest, especially New Mexico, were annexed into the United States?
10) What language, in addition to English, is spoken in northern New Mexico?
11) How can Jackson's marriage best be described?
12) What are Jackson's feelings about his marital situation?
13) What are Jackson's feelings about other women?
14) How does Jackson meet Ariel and what does she do for a living?
15) What does Ariel think about Jackson's focus on the protester story?
16) Who is the primary leader and organizer of the land grant protest?
17) What does she do for a living and what is her relationship to the protest?
18) Who has current title to the land claimed by the protester?
19) Is the protest resolved peacefully?
20) Do the protesters ultimately obtain grazing land for their sheep?

www.ingramcontent.com/pod-product-compliance
Lightning Source LLC
Chambersburg PA
CBHW010746310726
48980CB00004B/375

* 9 7 8 1 6 3 2 9 3 6 3 7 0 *